JUSTICE FOR ALL!

A GOLDEN BOOK • NEW YORK

DC COMICS™

Copyright © 2016 DC Comics.
DC SUPER FRIENDS and all related characters and
elements are trademarks of and © DC Comics.
WB SHIELD: ™ & © Warner Bros. Entertainment Inc.
(s16)

RHUS35667

ISBN 978-1-101-93151-6

randomhousekids.com

MANUFACTURED IN CHINA

10 9 8 7 6 5 4 3 2 1

We are the Super Friends!

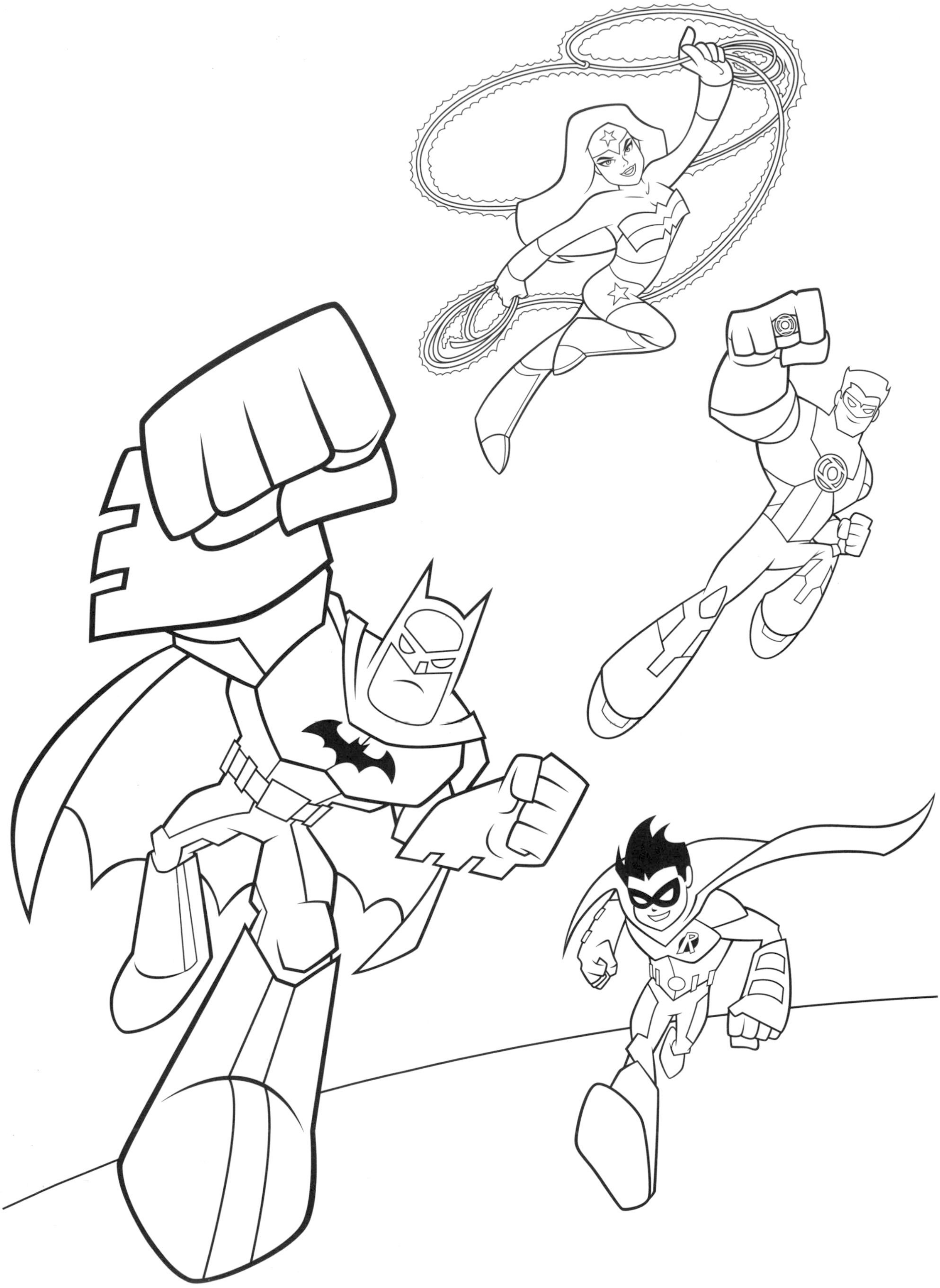

We fight for truth and justice!

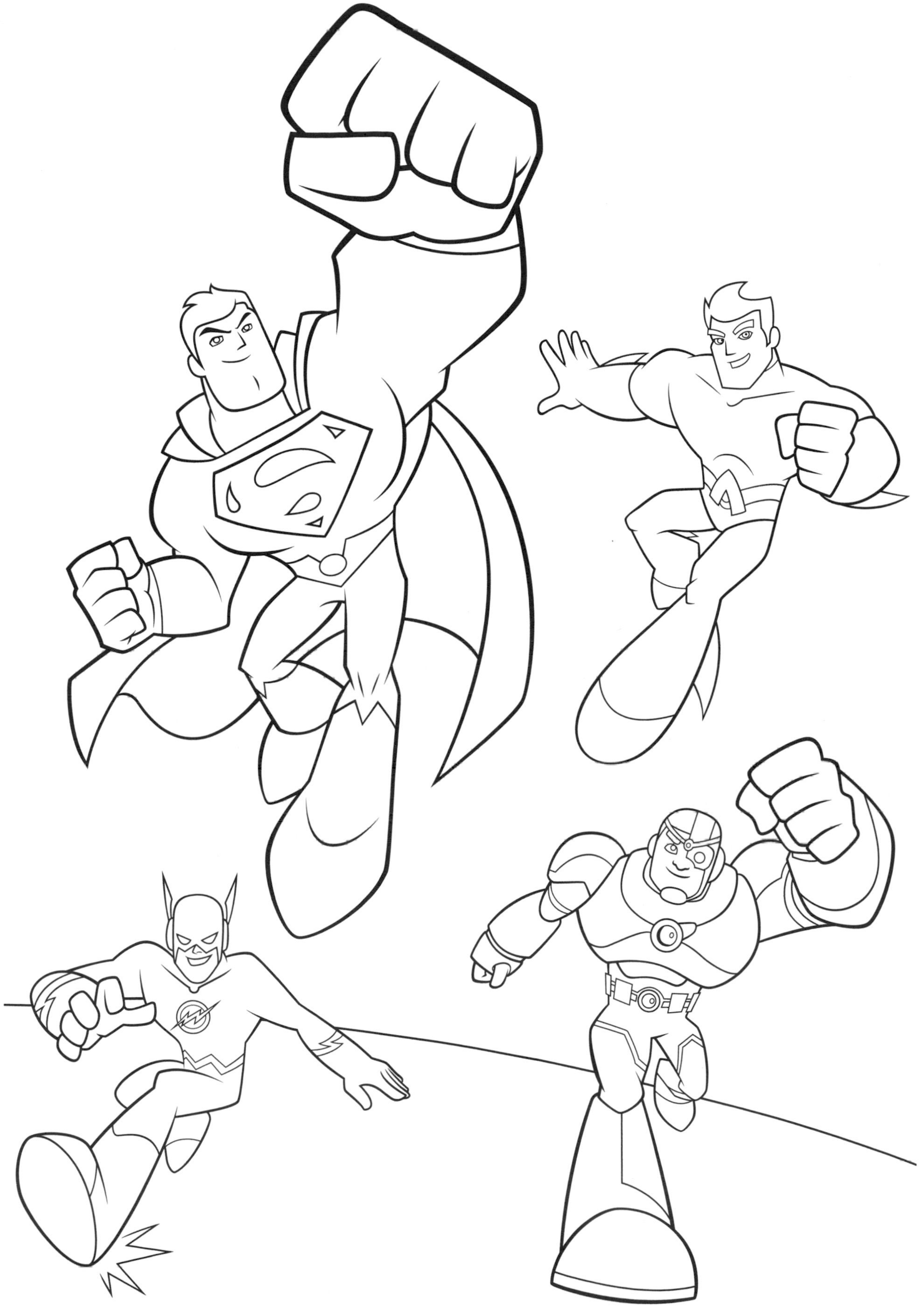

SUPERMAN!

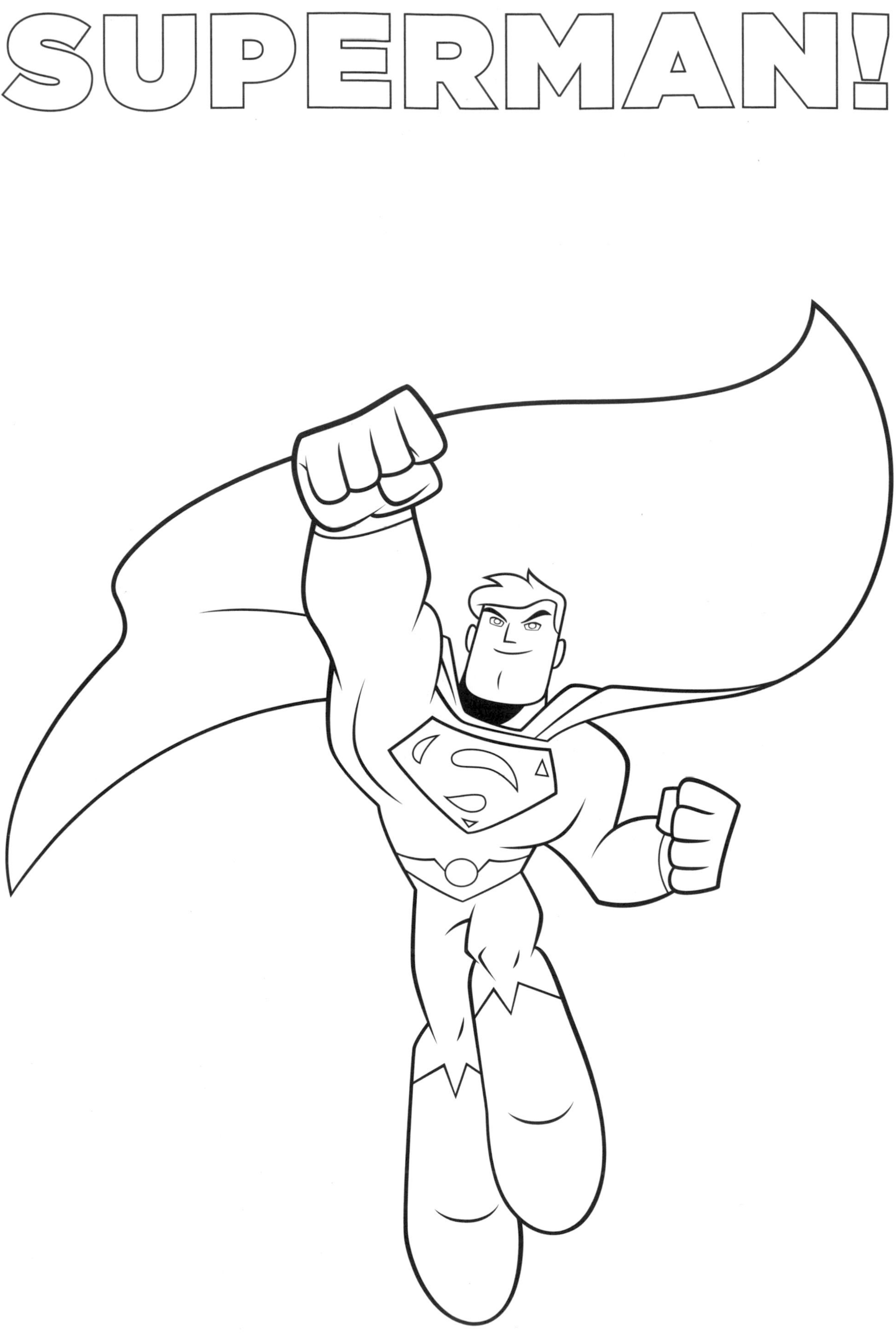

WONDER WOMAN!

BATMAN!

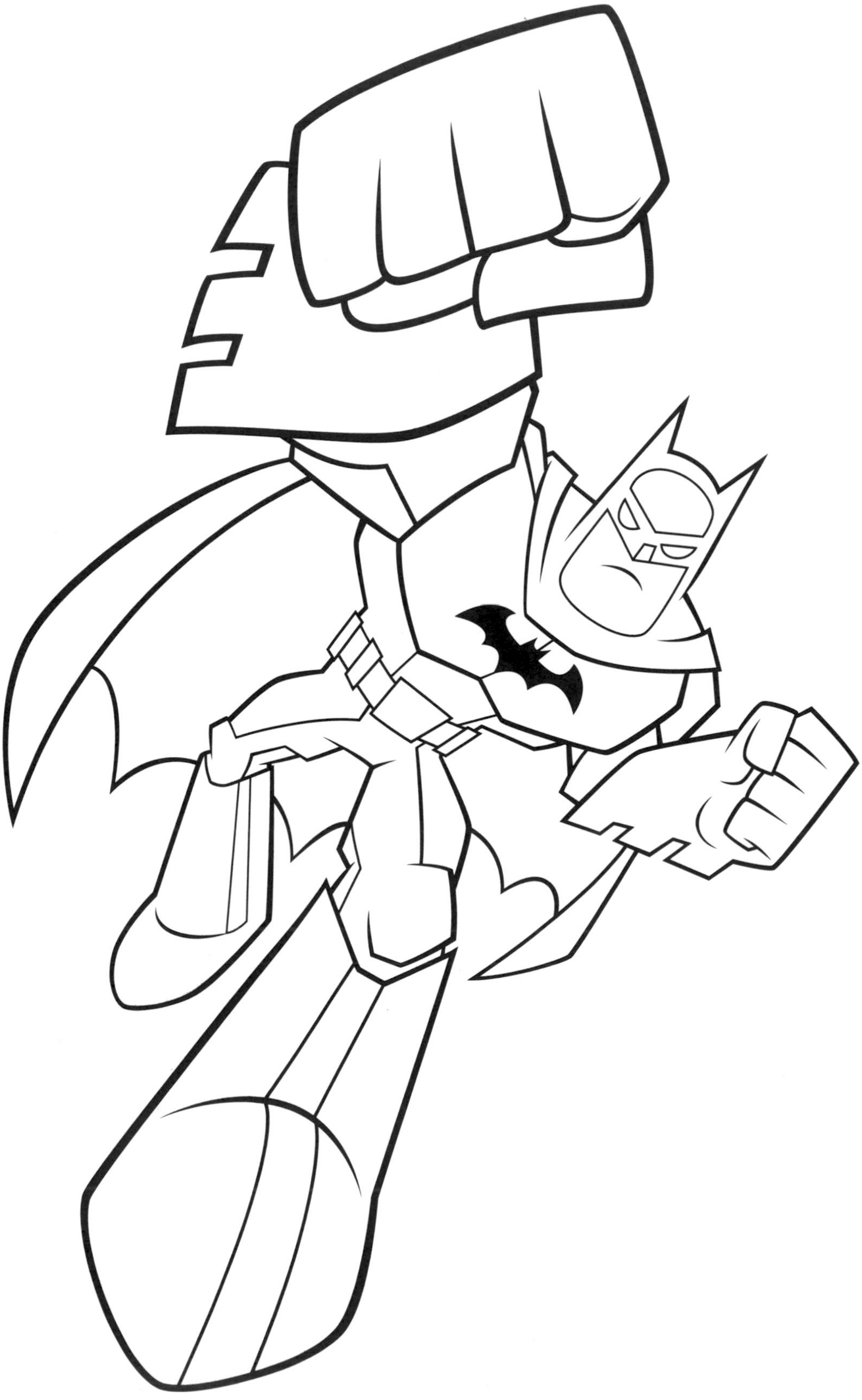

ROBIN!

THE FLASH!

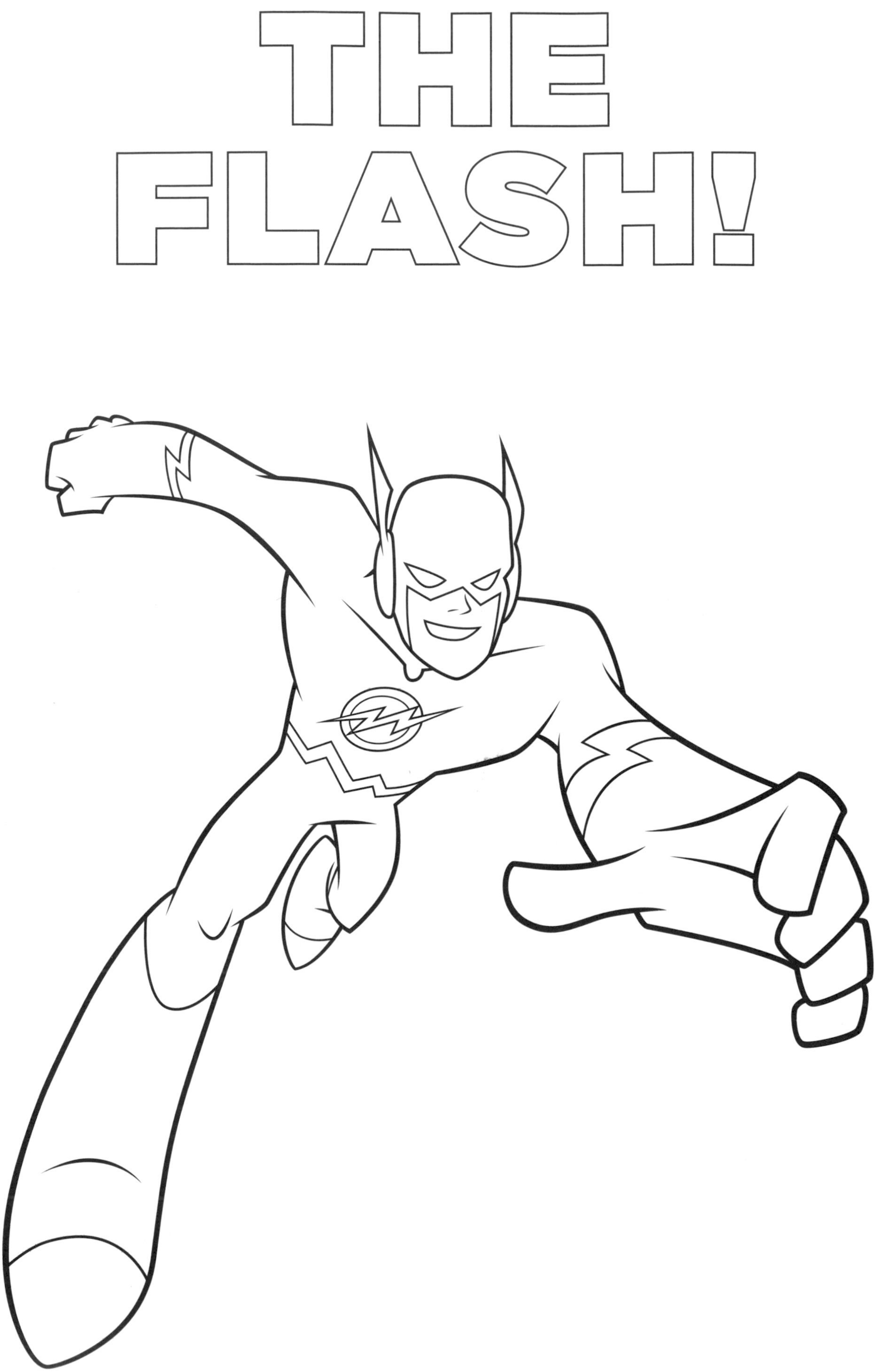

GREEN LANTERN!

AQUAMAN!

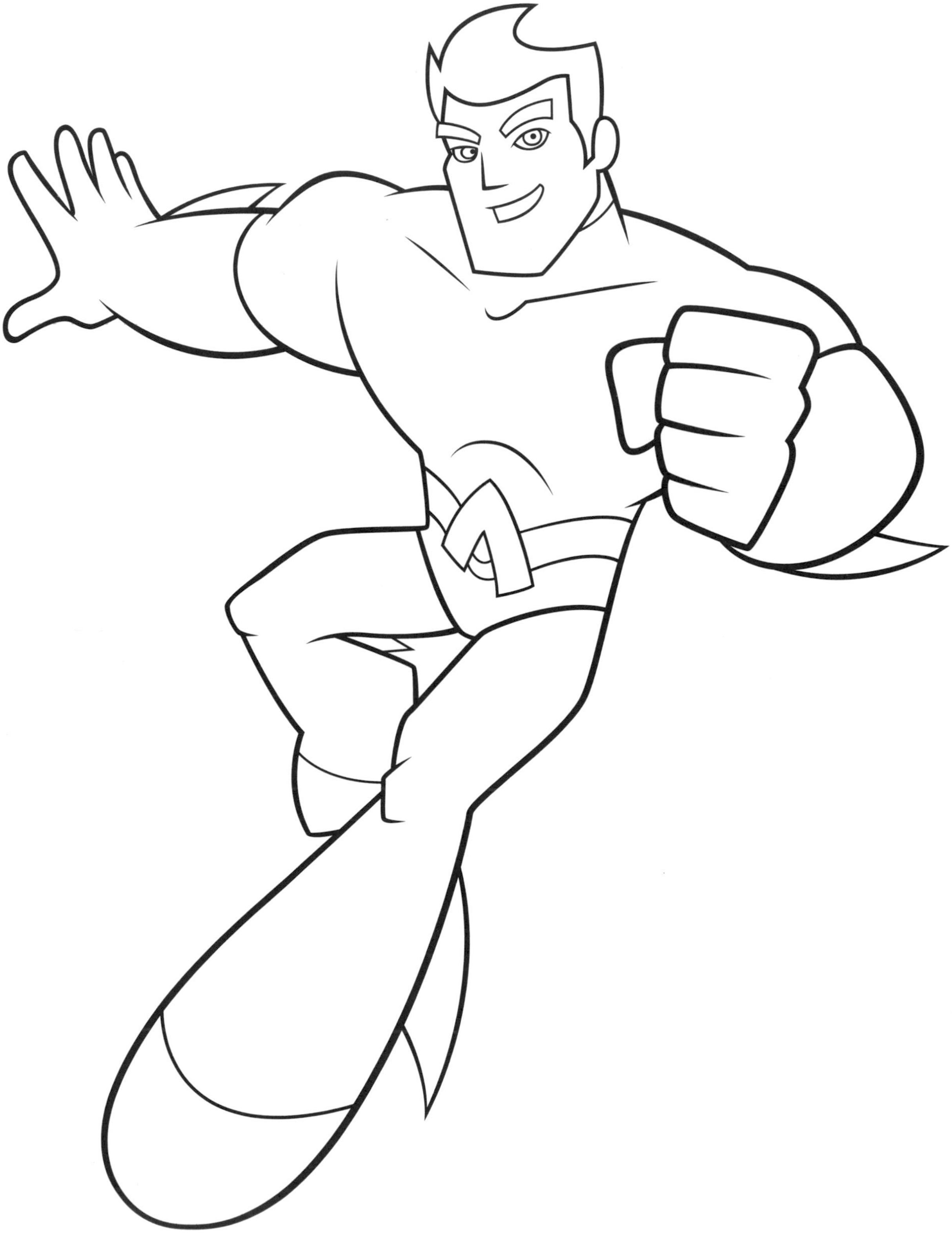

CYBORG!

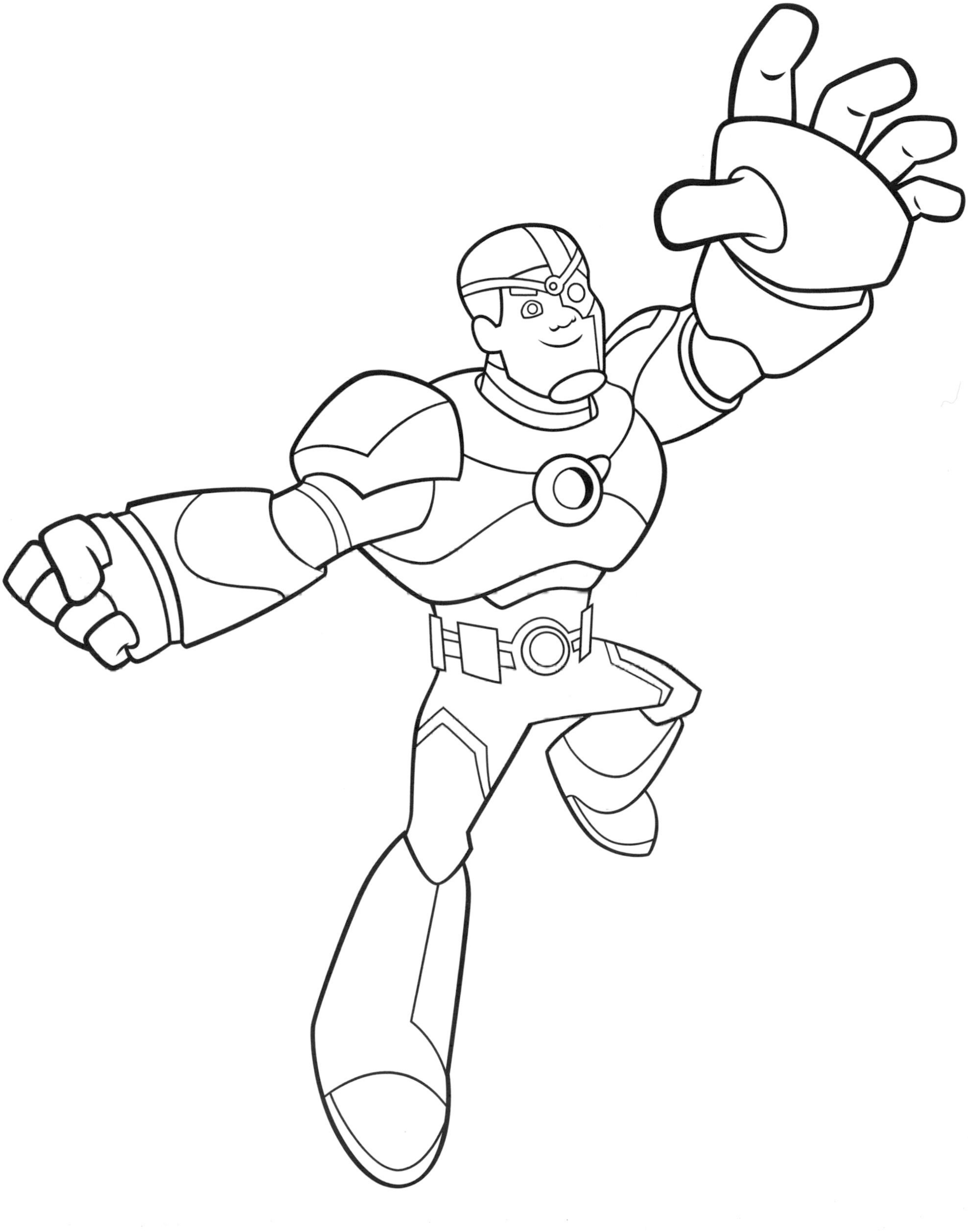

HAWKMAN!

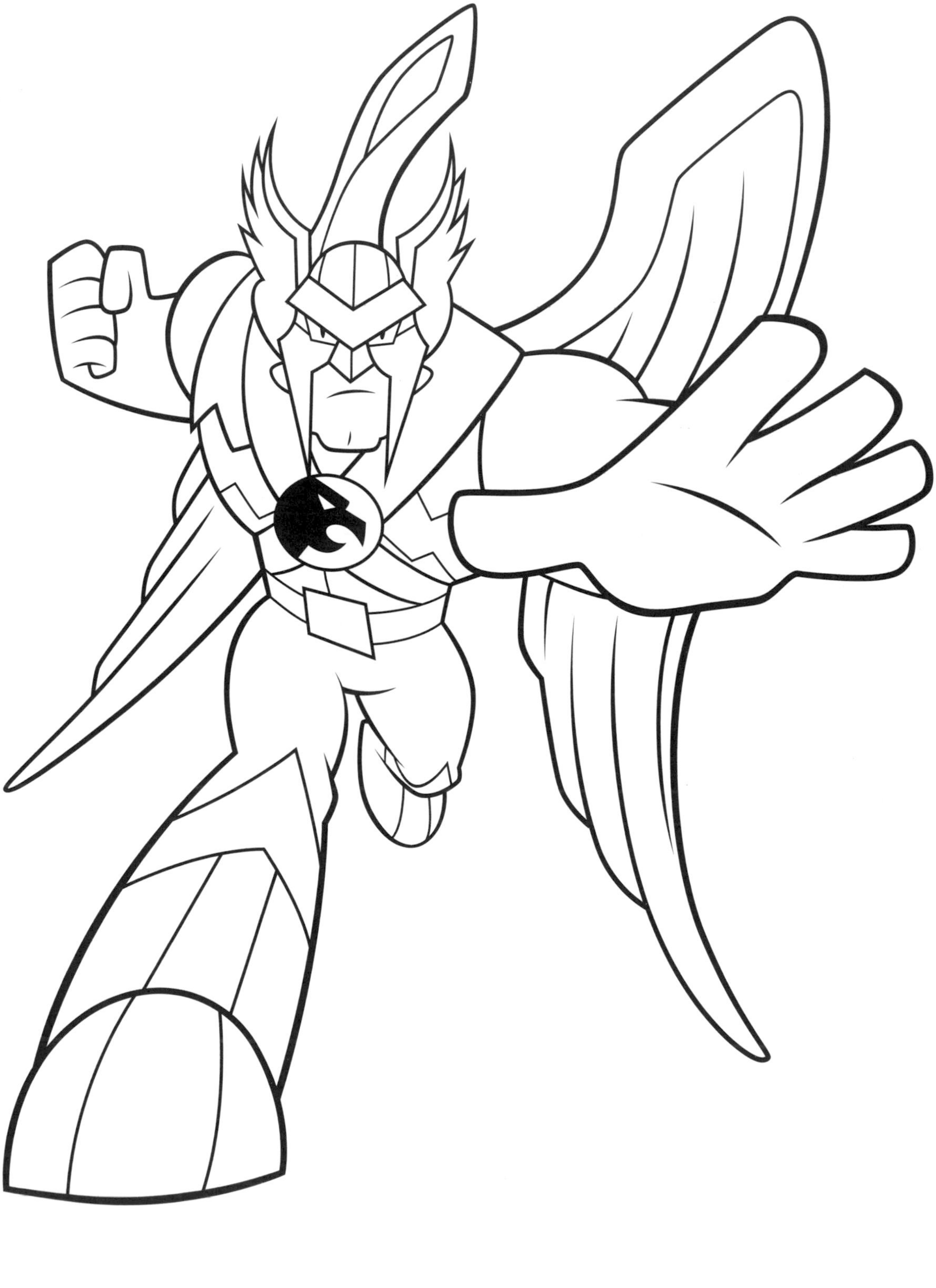

Draw a line from each picture to its close-up.

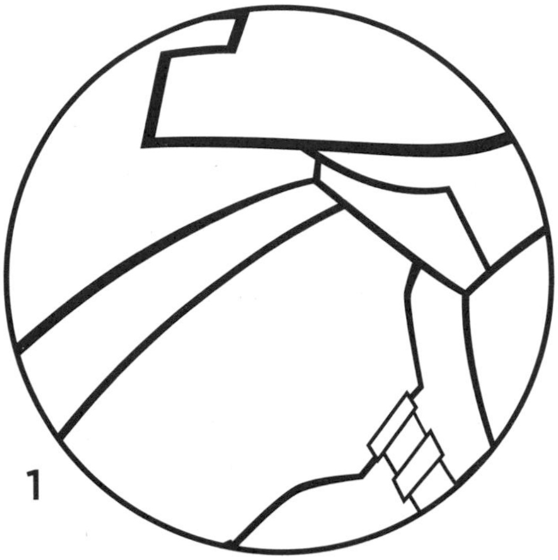

1

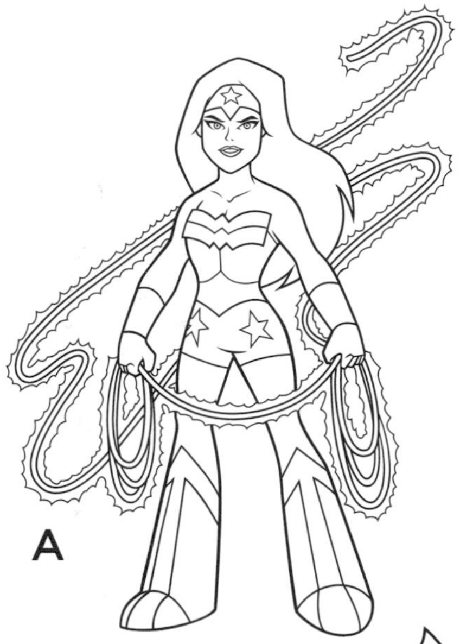

A

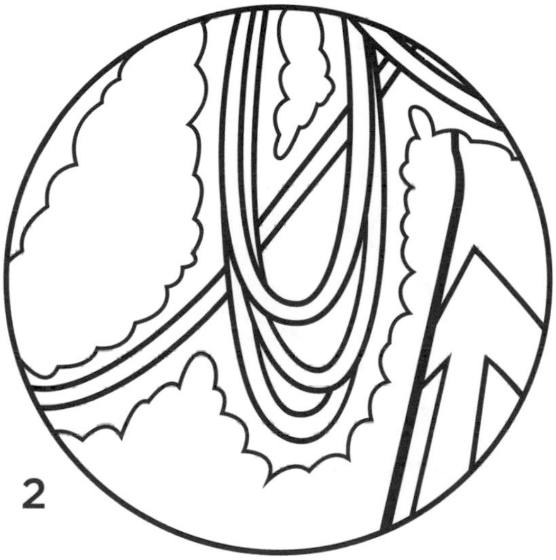

2

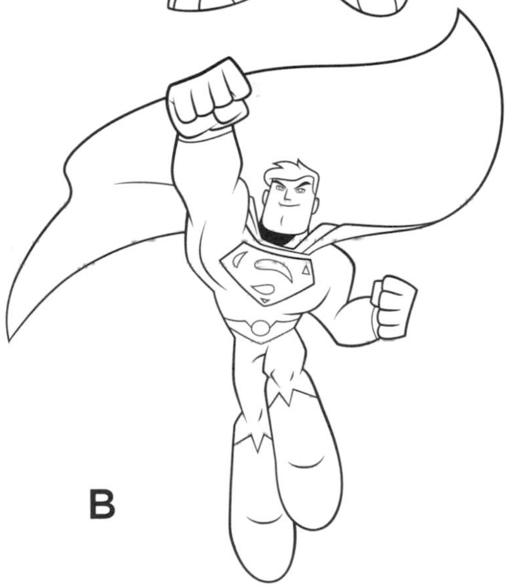

B

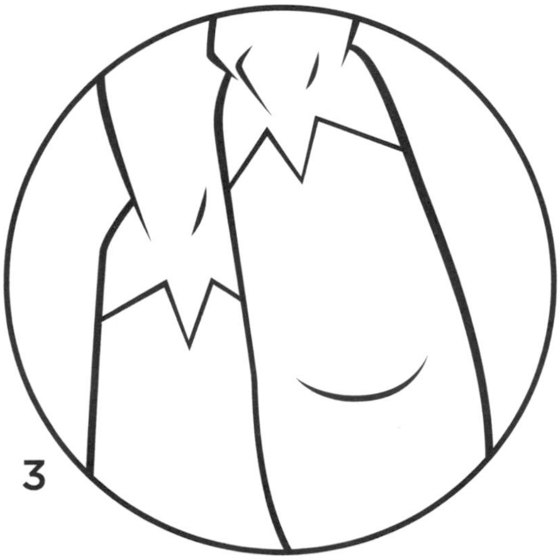

3

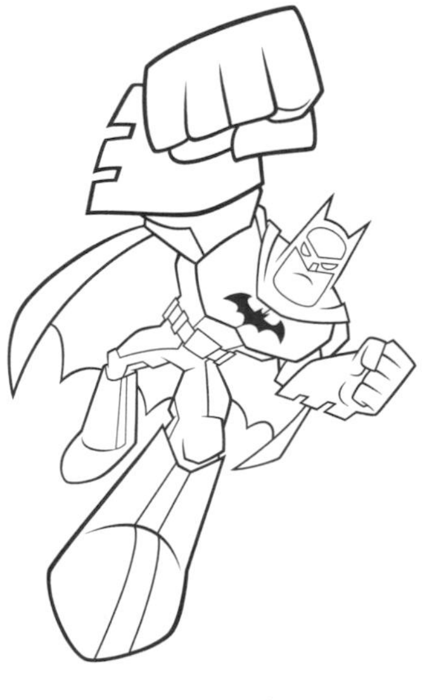

C

ANSWER: 1-C; 2-A; and 3-B.

To find out Superman's nickname, follow the lines and write each letter in the correct box.

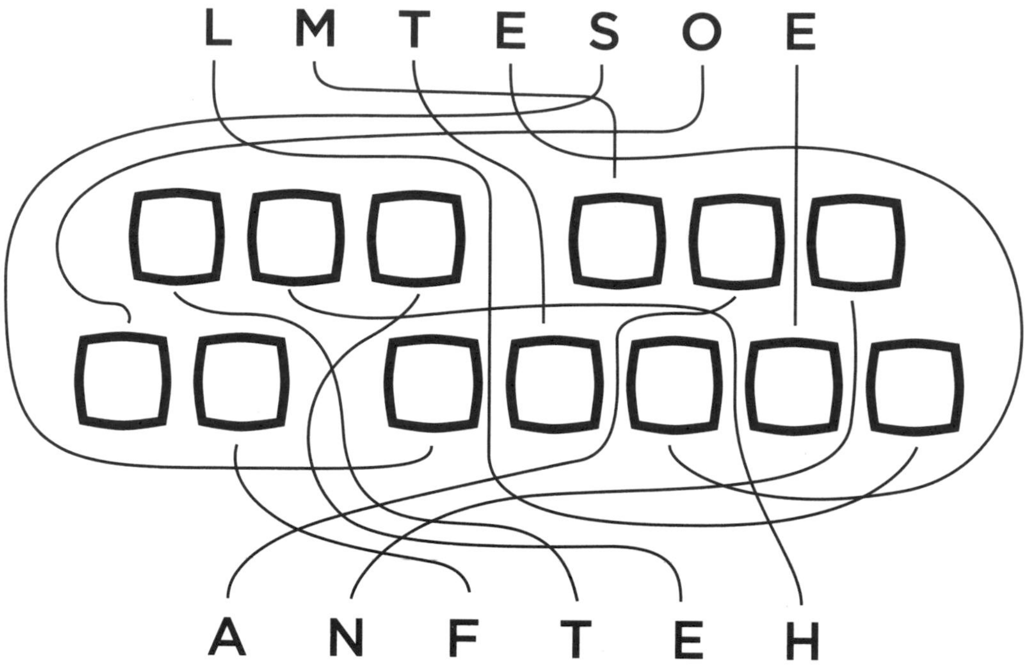
L M T E S O E
A N F T E H

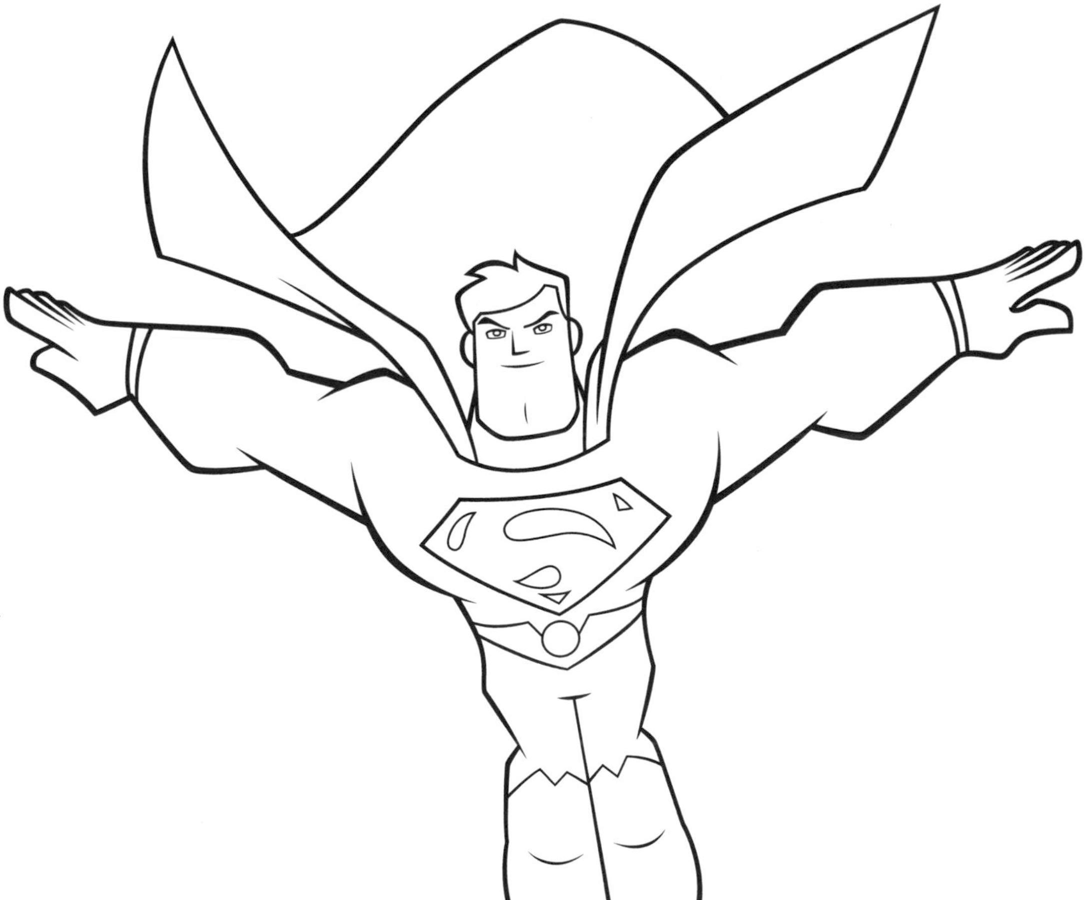

ANSWER: The Man of Steel.

Lex Luthor is an evil genius. He will do almost anything to defeat Superman!

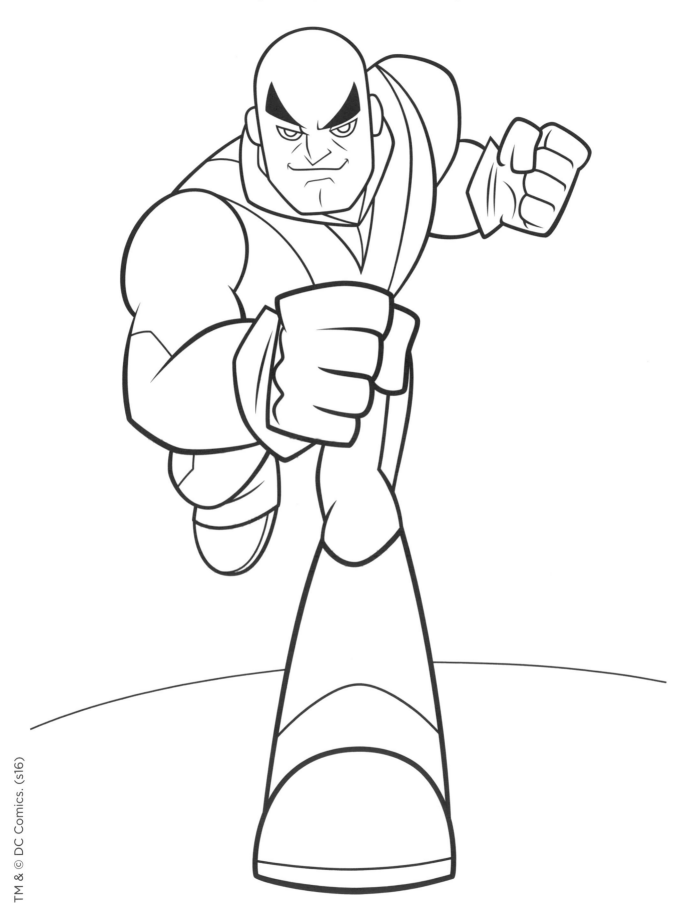

Circle the picture of Lex that is different from the others.

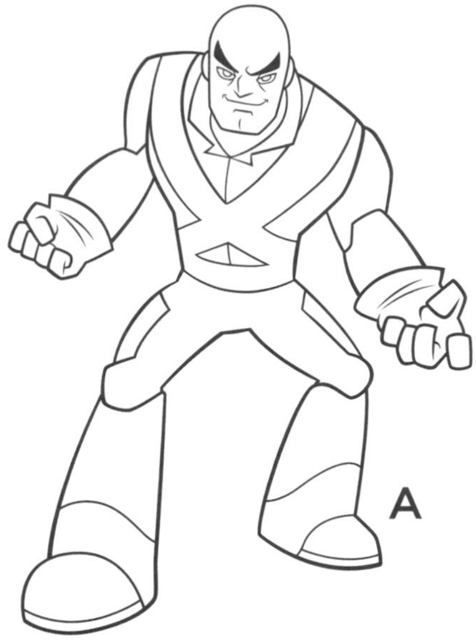

A

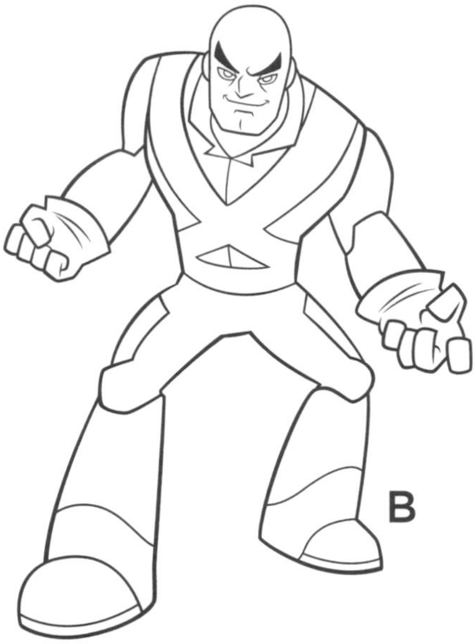

B

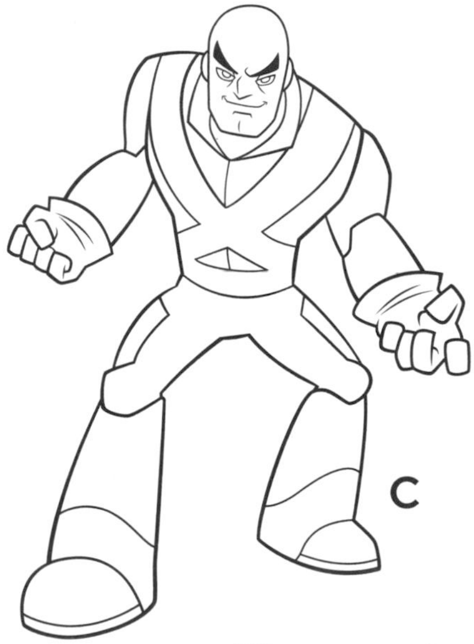

C

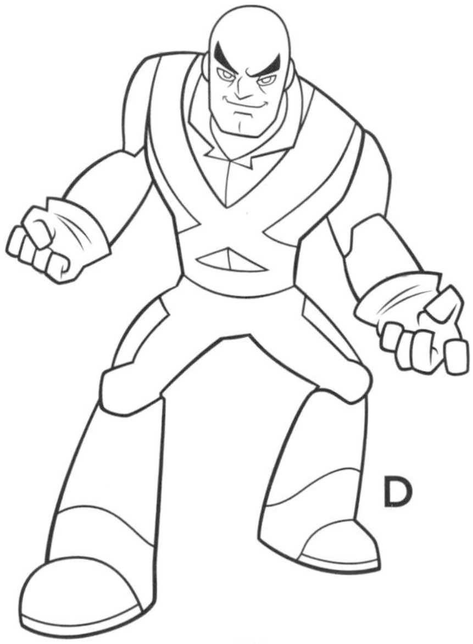

D

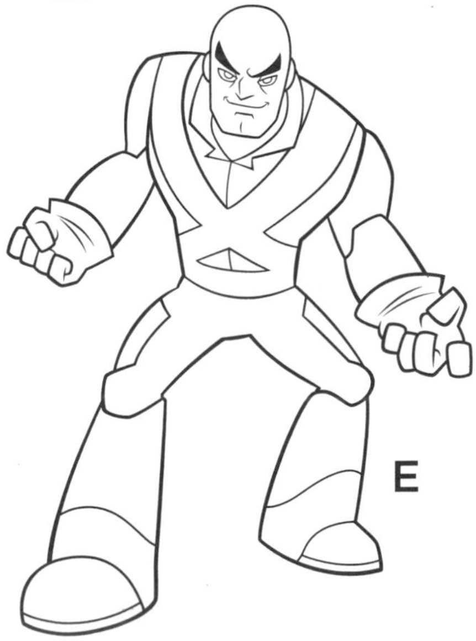

E

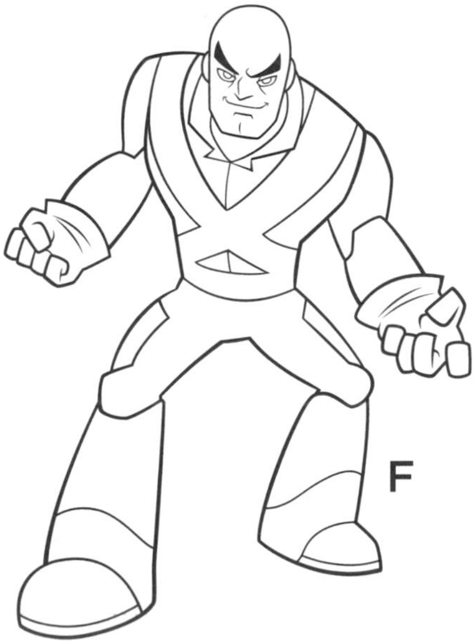

F

ANSWER: C.

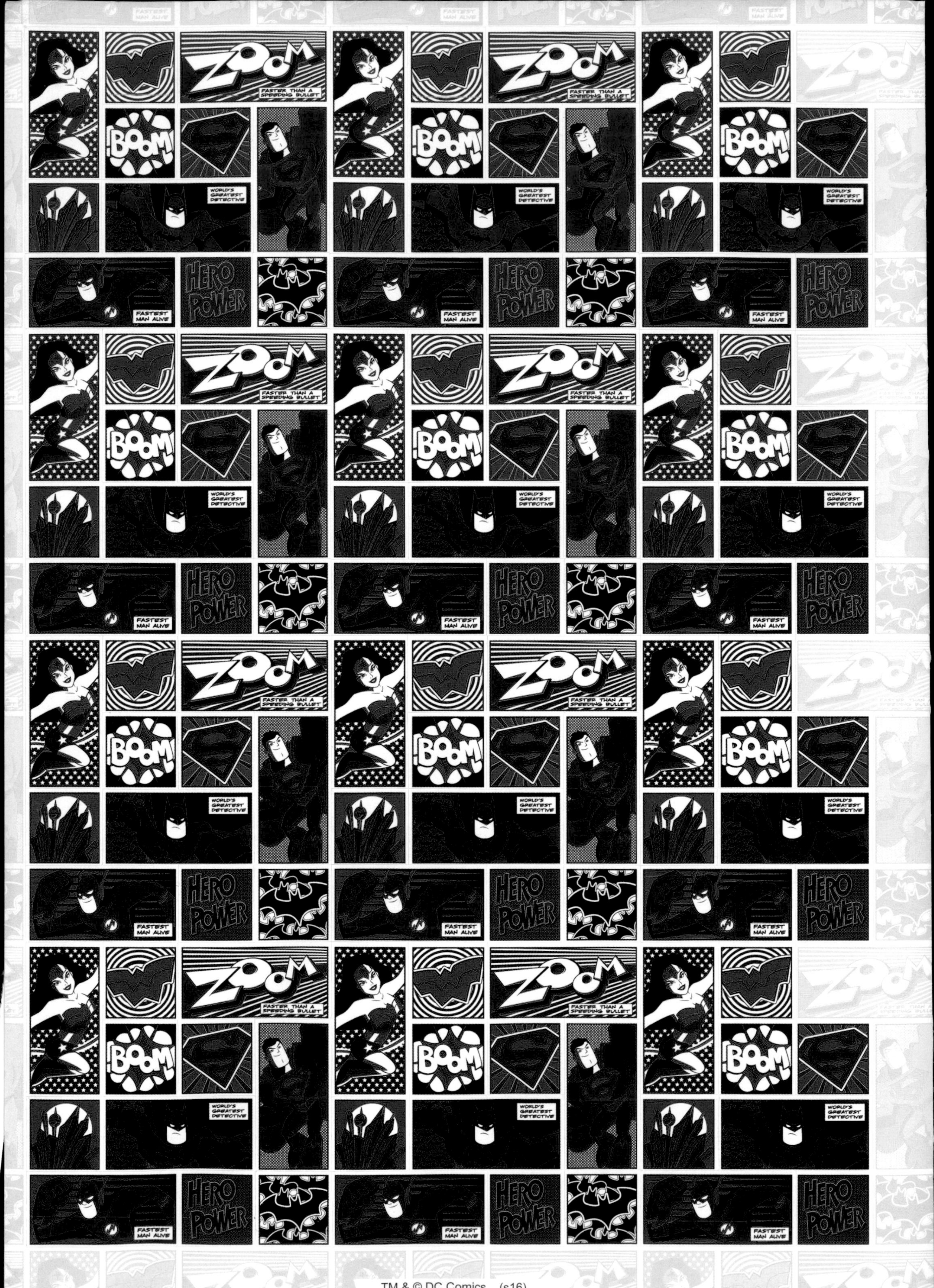
ZOOM
FASTER THAN A SPEEDING BULLET
BOOM!
WORLD'S GREATEST DETECTIVE
HERO POWER
FASTEST MAN ALIVE

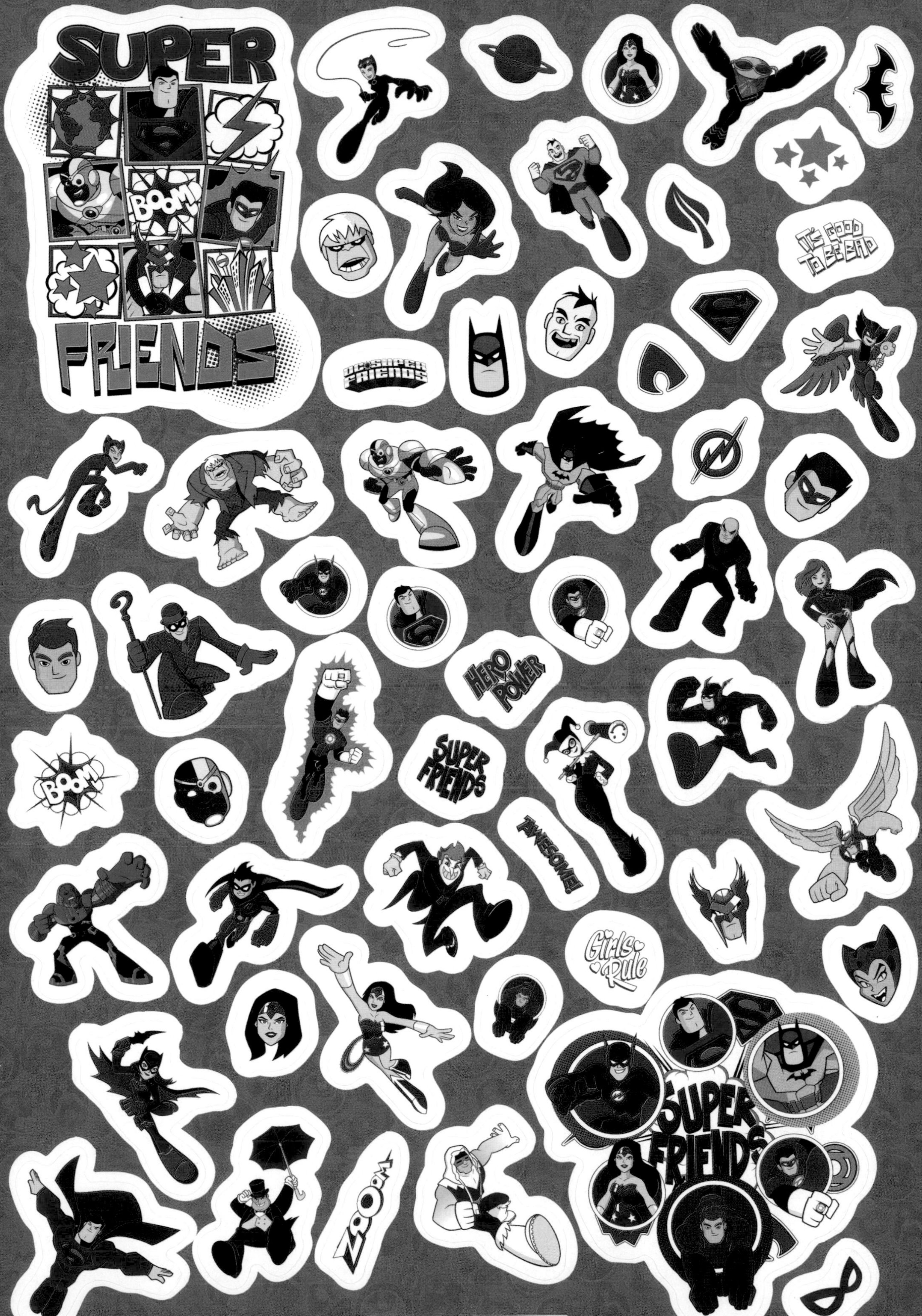
SUPER
BOOM
FRIENDS
DC SUPER FRIENDS
IT'S GOOD TO BE BAD
HERO POWER
BOOM
SUPER FRIENDS
AWESOME!
Girls Rule
ZOOOM
SUPER FRIENDS

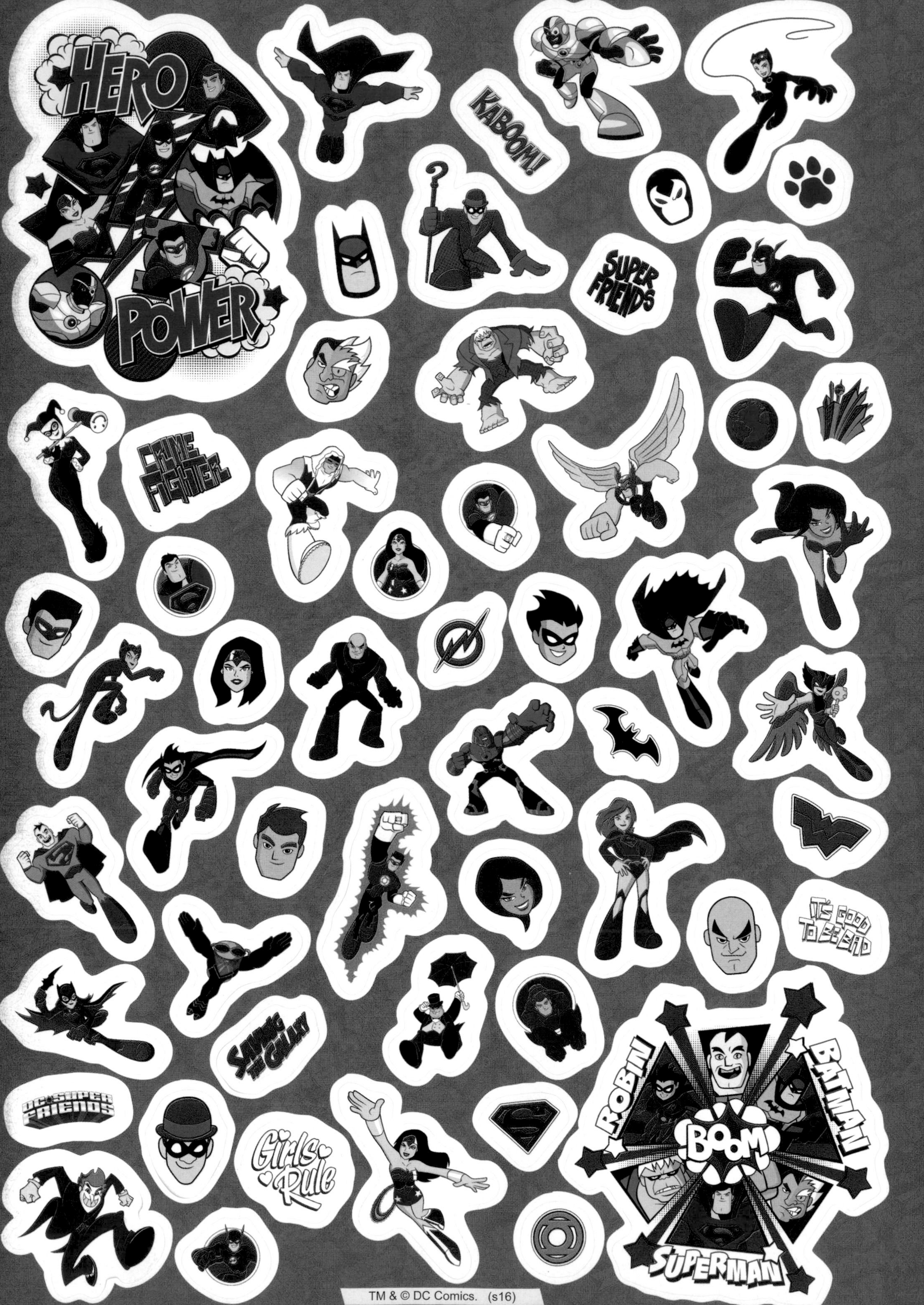
HERO
POWER
KABOOM!
SUPER FRIENDS
CRIME FIGHTER
IT'S GOOD TO BE BAD
SAVING THE GALAXY
DC SUPER FRIENDS
Girls Rule
ROBIN
BATMAN
BOOM
SUPERMAN

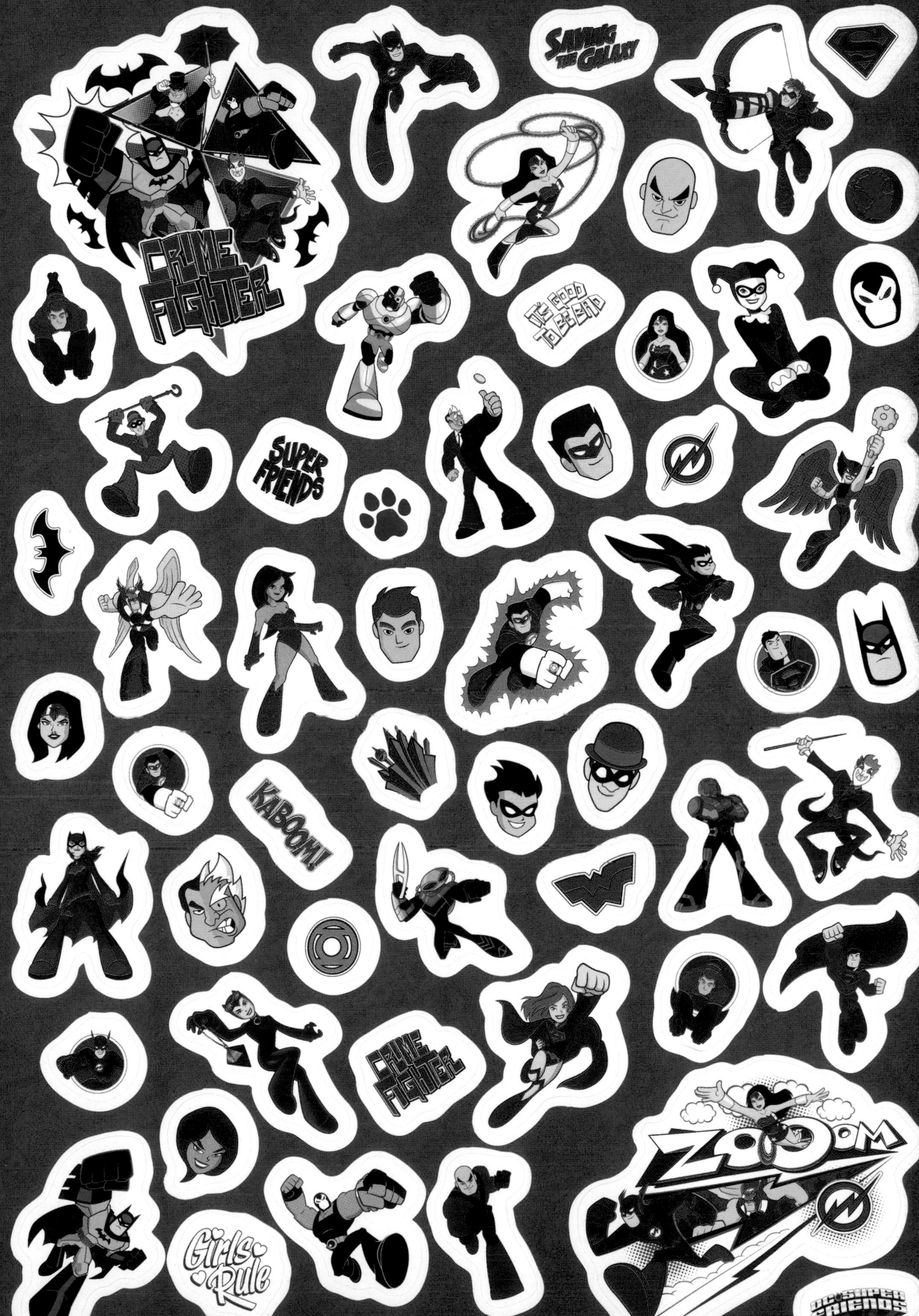
Saving the Galaxy
Crime Fighter
It's good to be bad
Super Friends
Kaboom!
Crime Fighter
Zoom
Girls Rule
DC Super Friends

Help Superman solve the maze by following the path of Lex Luthor pictures.

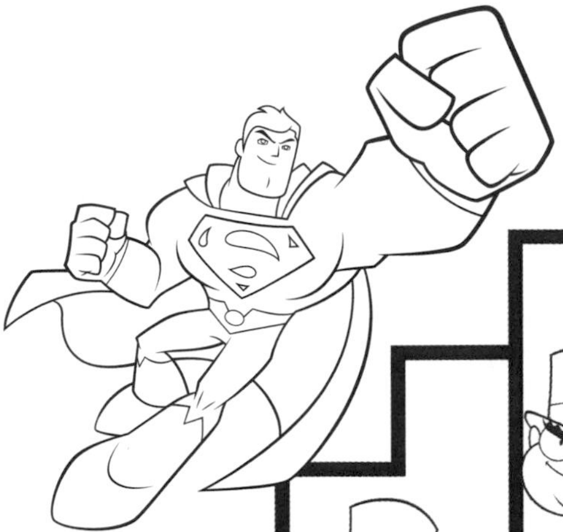

START

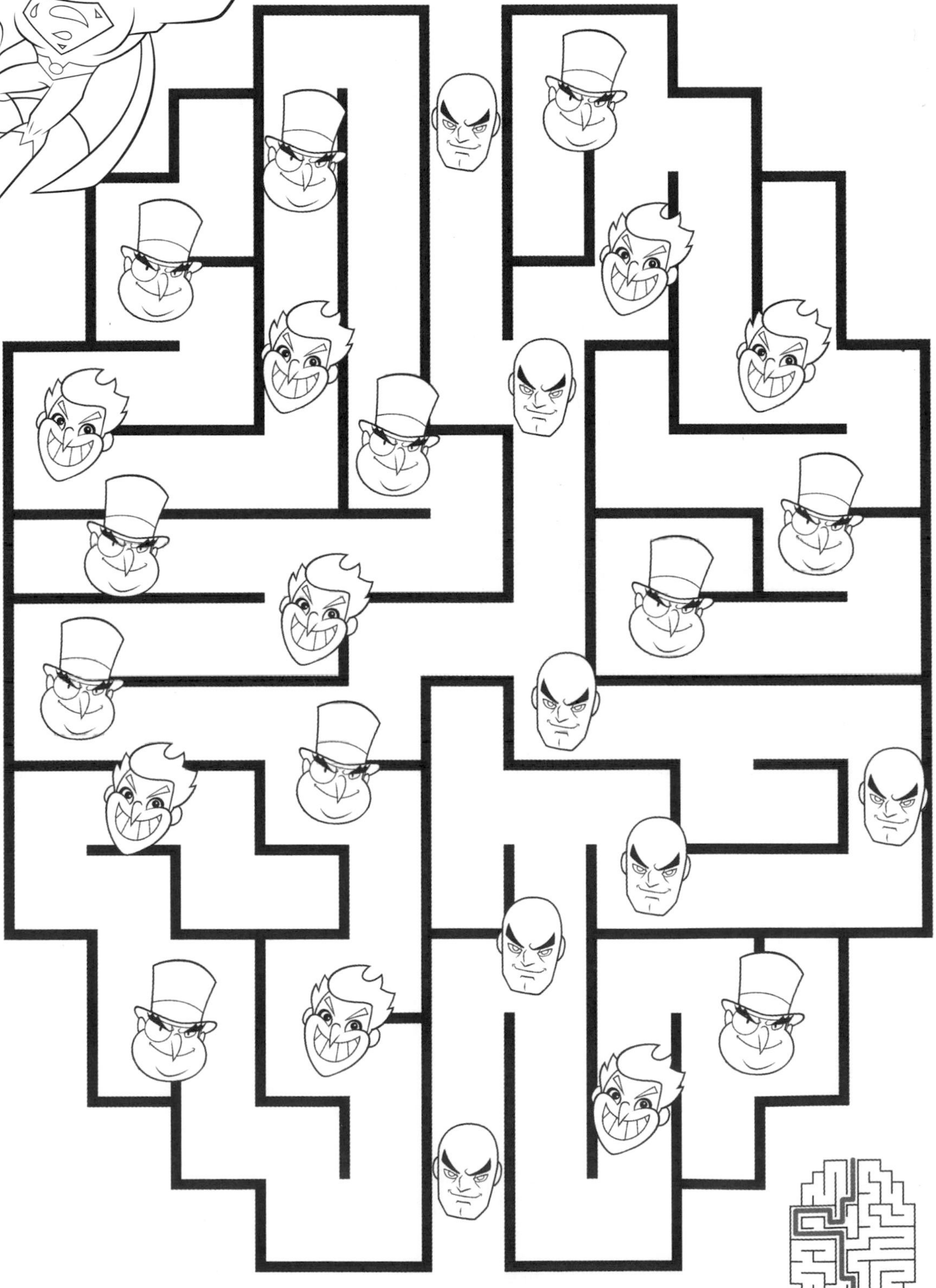

FINISH

ANSWER:

**How many times can you find LEX in the puzzle?
Look up, down, forward, and backward.**

L	L	E	X	X
E	X	L	E	X
X	E	L	L	X

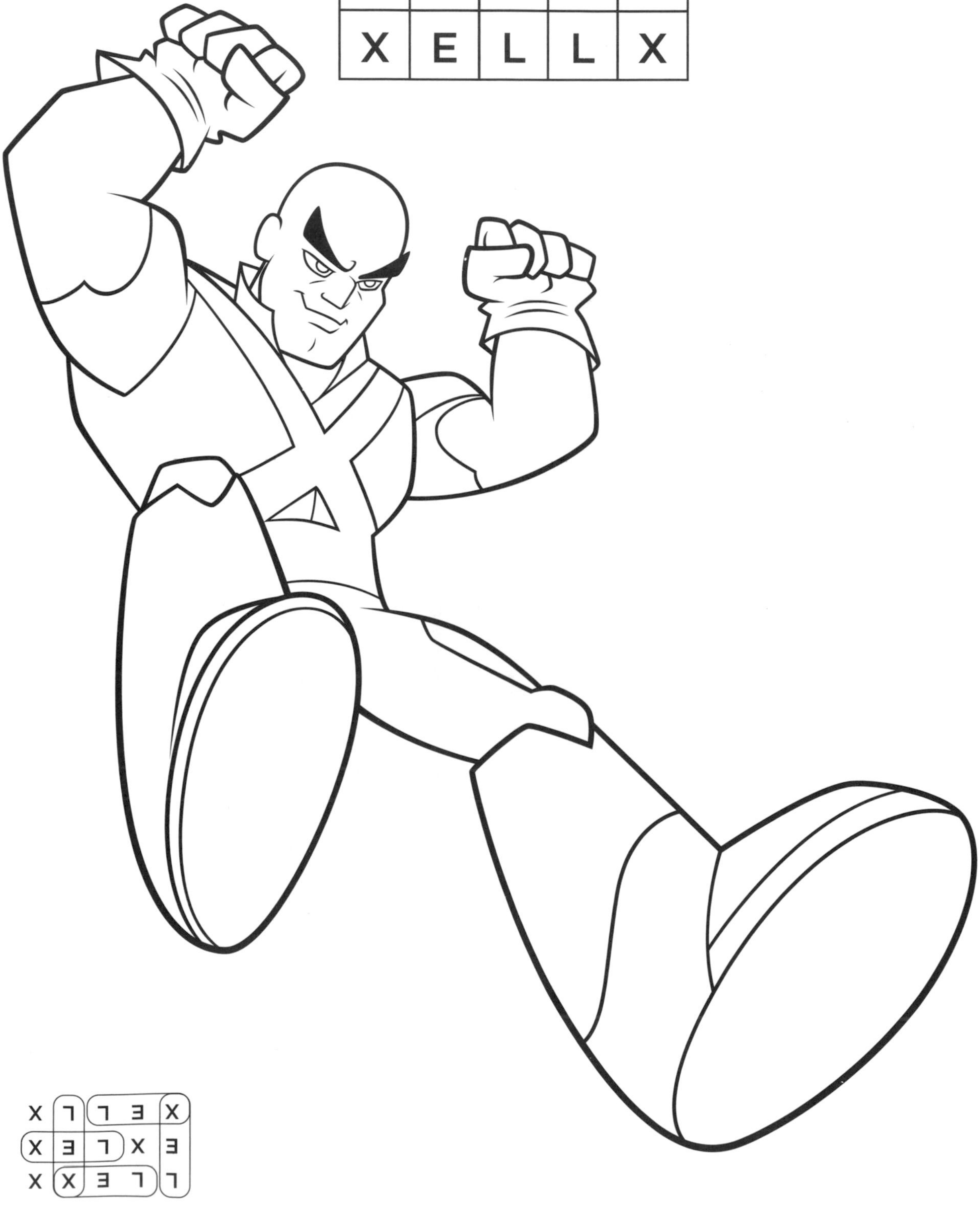

L	L	E	X	X
E	X	L	E	X
X	E	L	L	X

ANSWER: 5.

Wonder Woman is an Amazon princess. She is fearless!

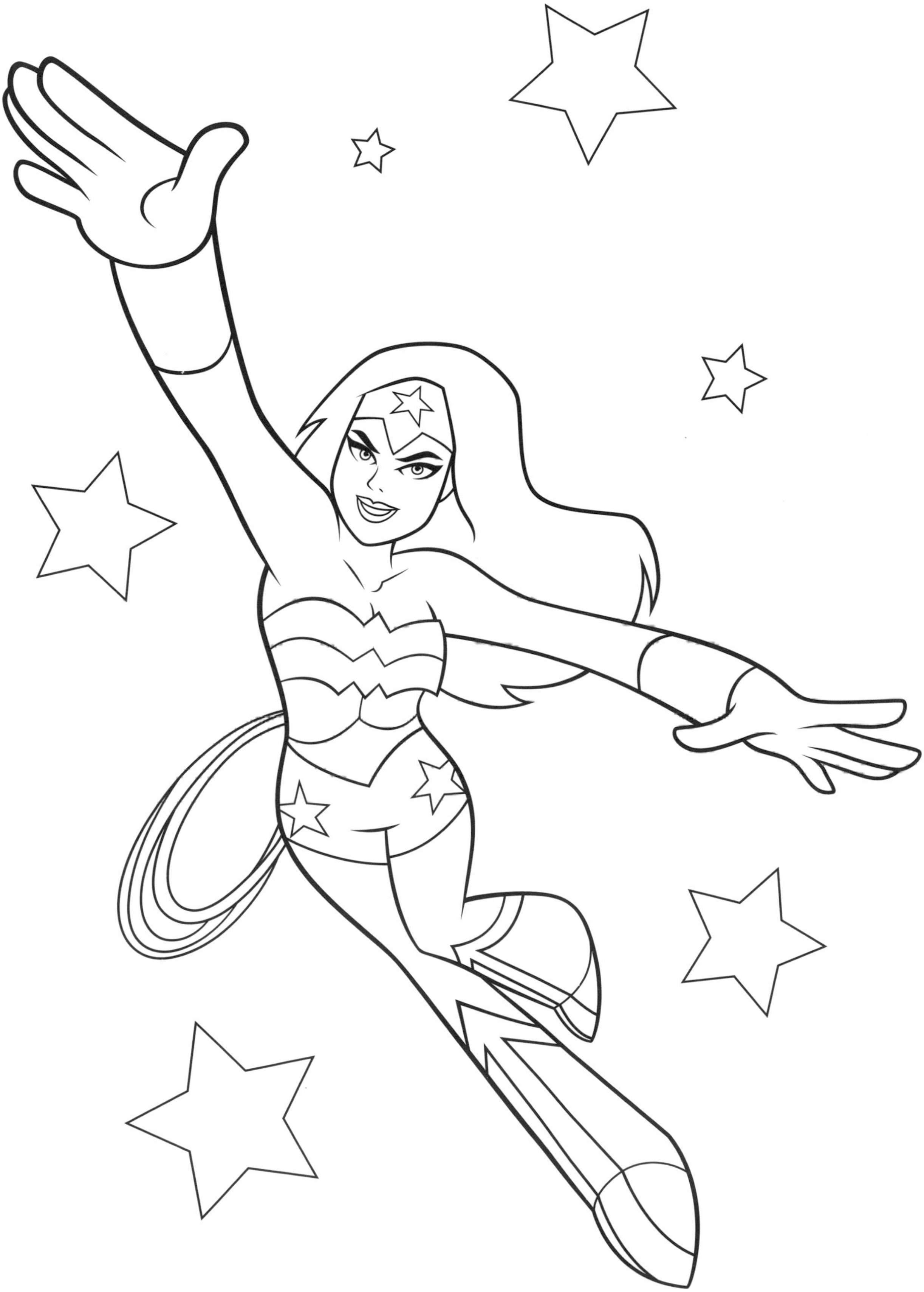

Use the grid to complete the picture of Wonder Woman.

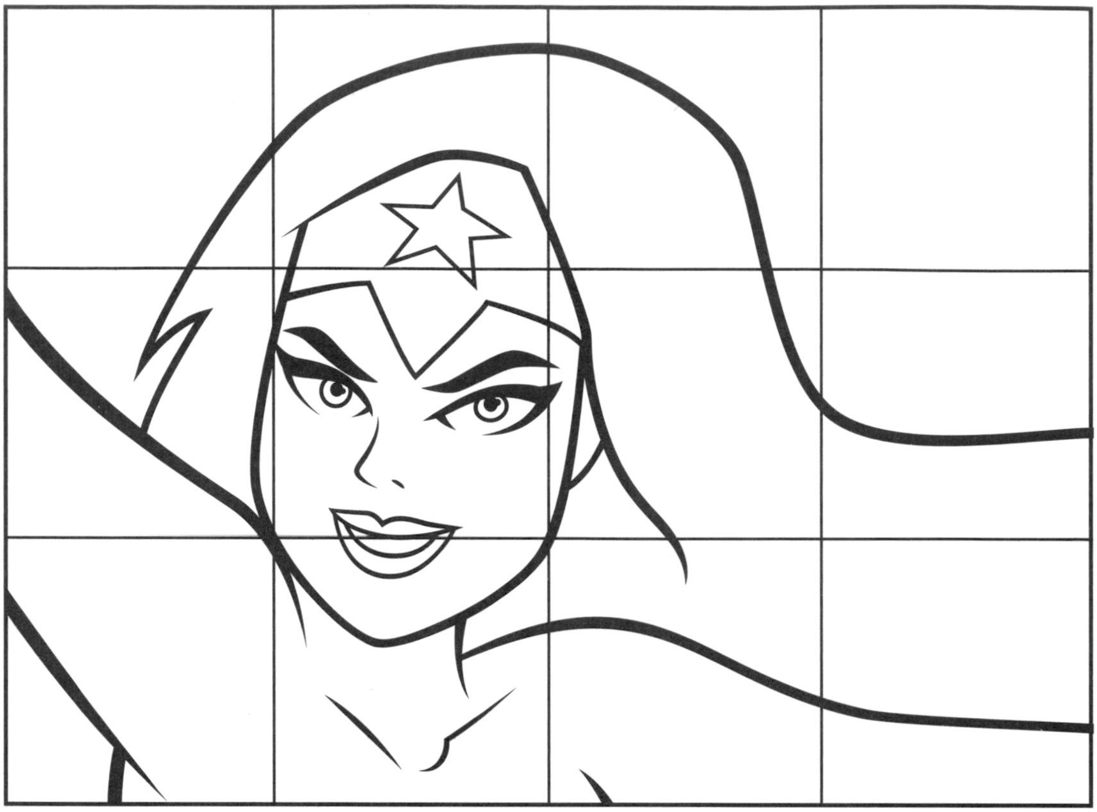

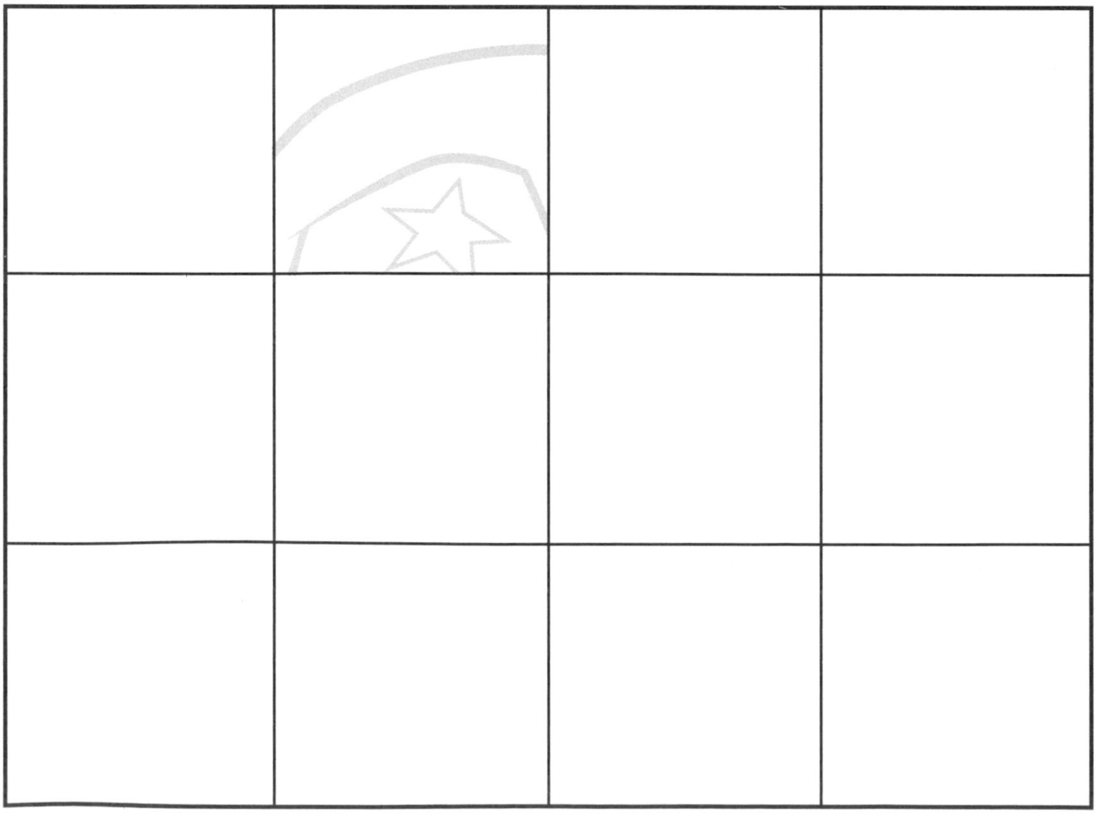

Use the code to find out the name of this villain.

A=1	C=2	E=3	H=4	T=5

__ __ __   __ __ __ __ __ __ __
5 4 3   2 4 3 3 5 1 4

The Cheetah can't wait to get her paws
on Wonder Woman's magic lasso!

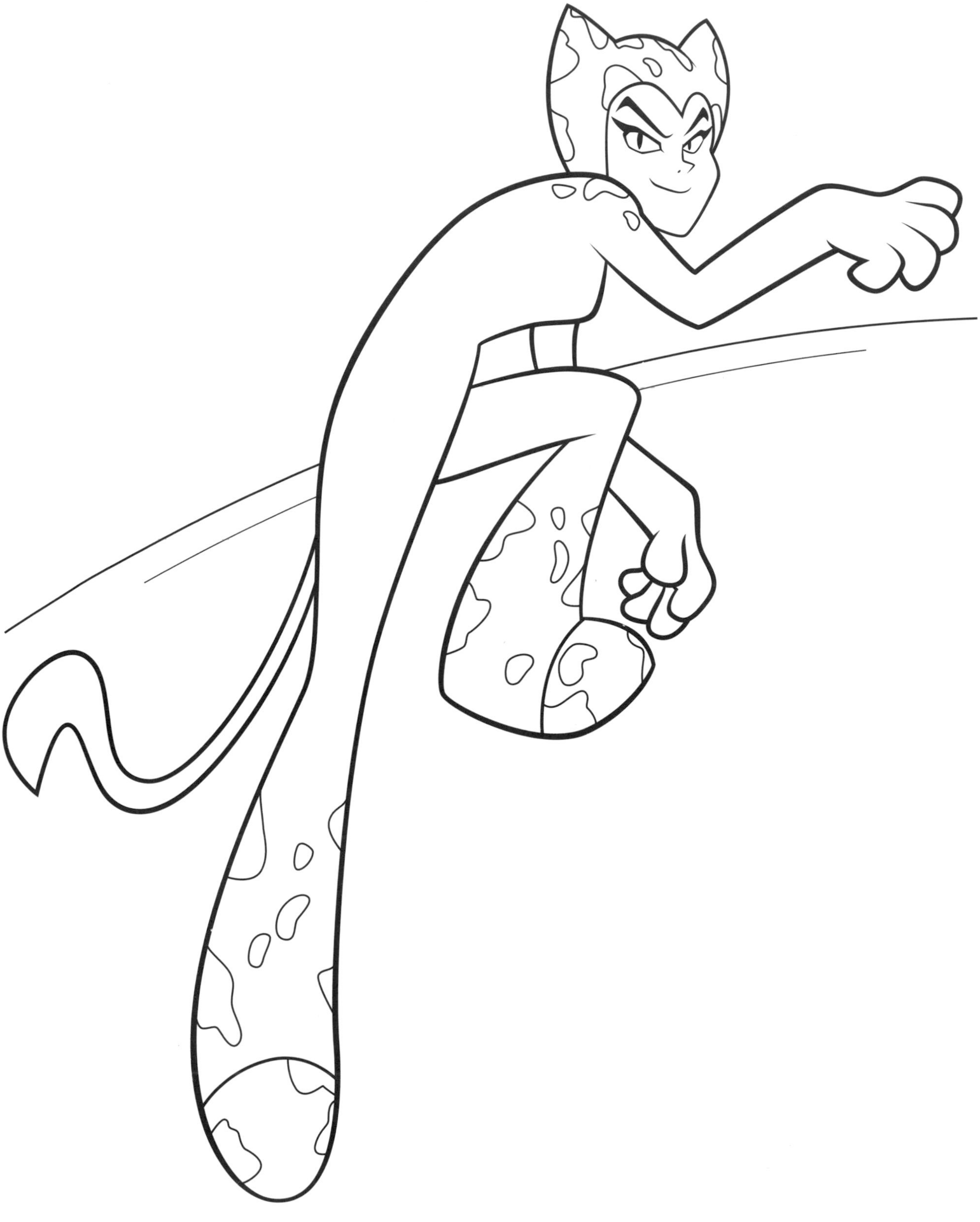

What is Batman’s nickname? To find out, follow the lines and write each letter in the correct box.

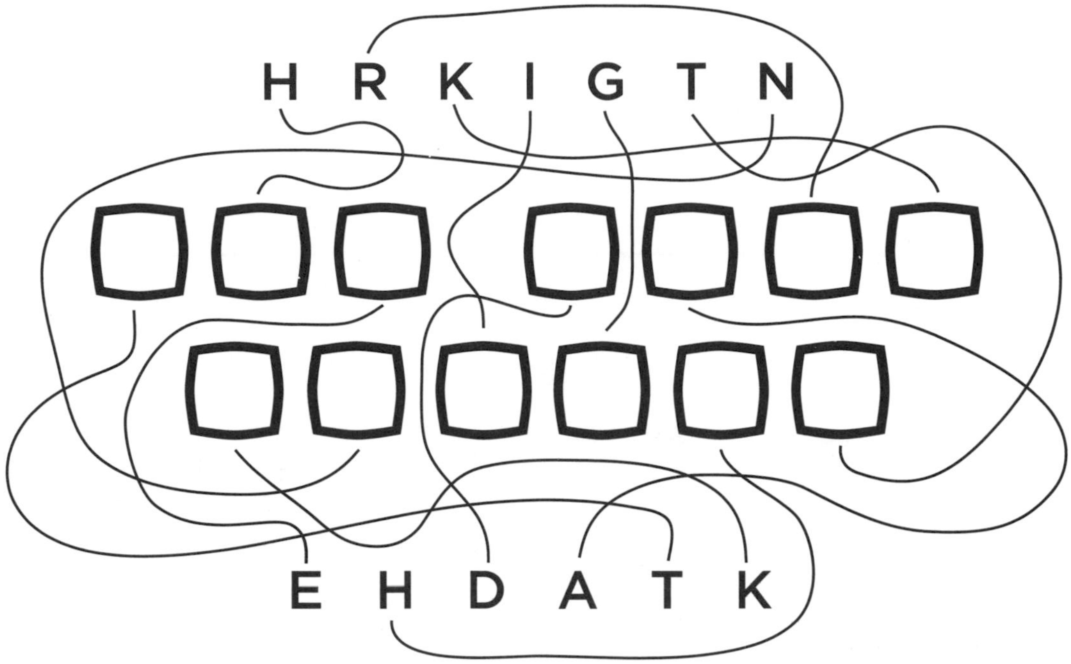
H R K I G T N
E H D A T K

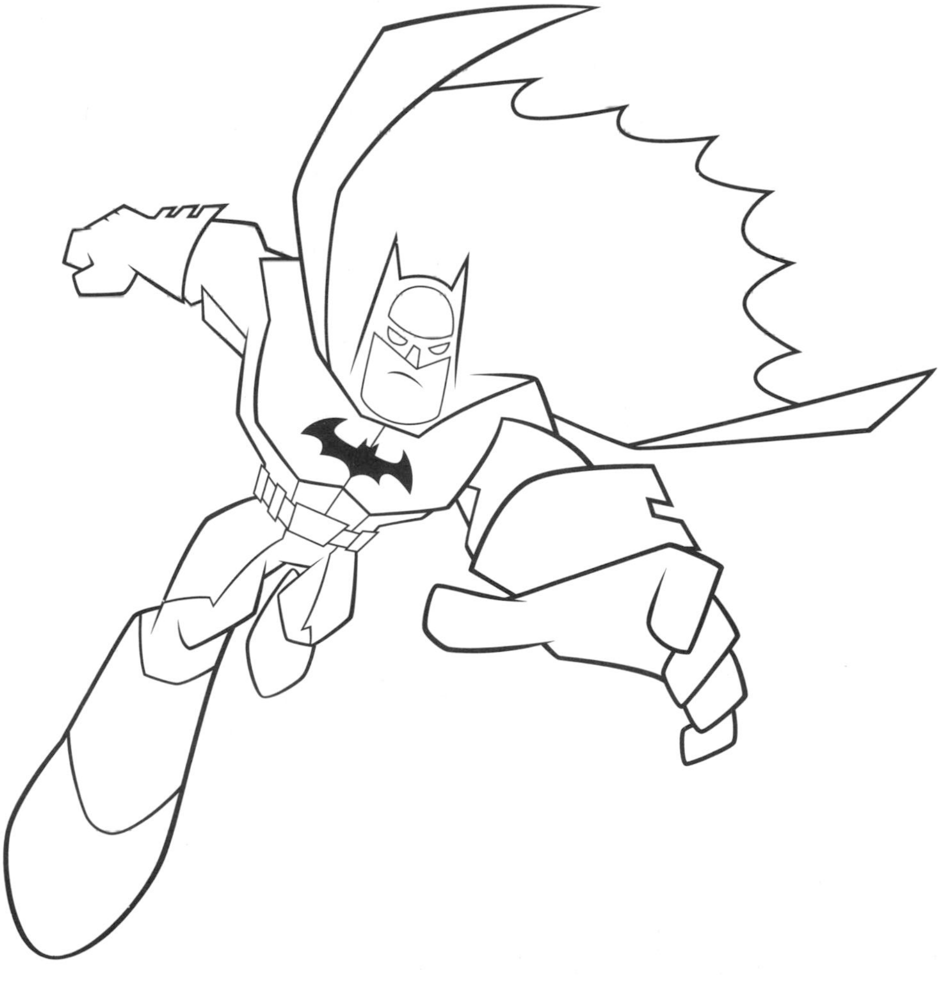

ANSWER: The Dark Knight.

Robin is Batman's partner. To find out his nickname, solve the maze. Then write the letters along the correct path in order on the blanks.

___ ___ ___   ___ ___ ___

___ ___ ___ ___ ___ ___

START
T
K
C
E
H
D
P
E
E
H
B
M
O
H
O
Y
E
T
W
O
F
D
S
T
K
N
M
L
E
D
E
O
R
P
FINISH

ANSWER: The Boy Wonder.

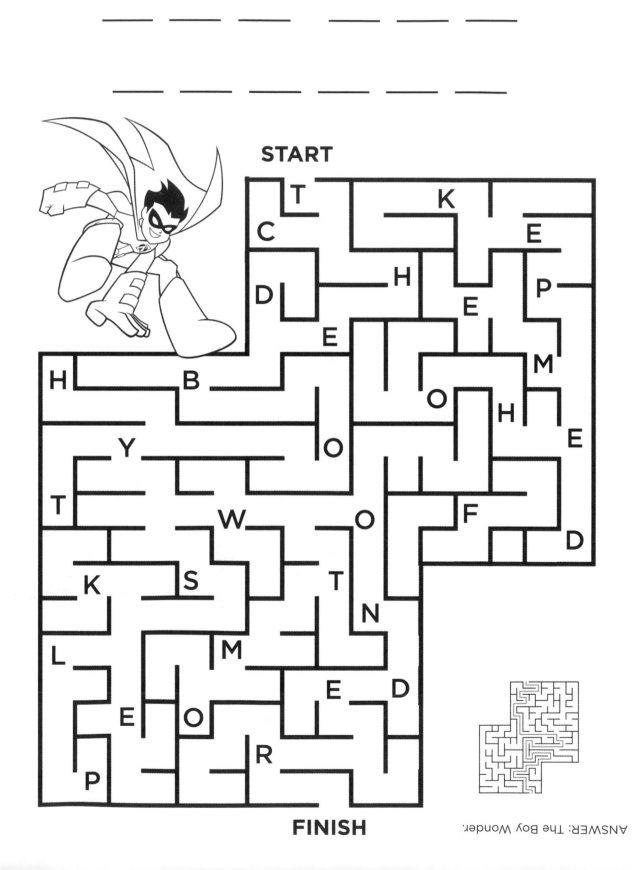

Batman and Robin are also known as the Dynamic Duo!

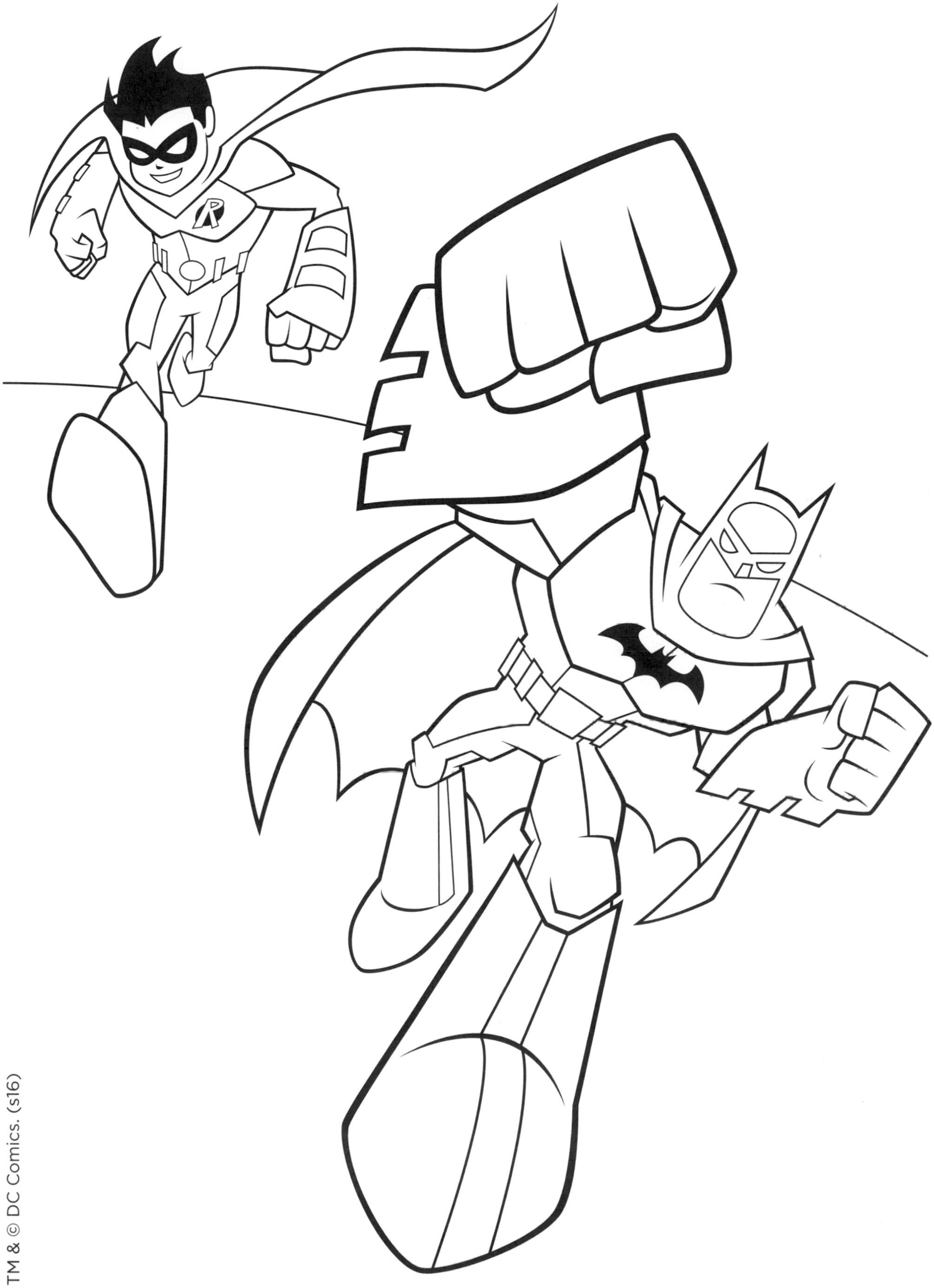

Solve the maze to help the Dynamic Duo find their friend Superman.

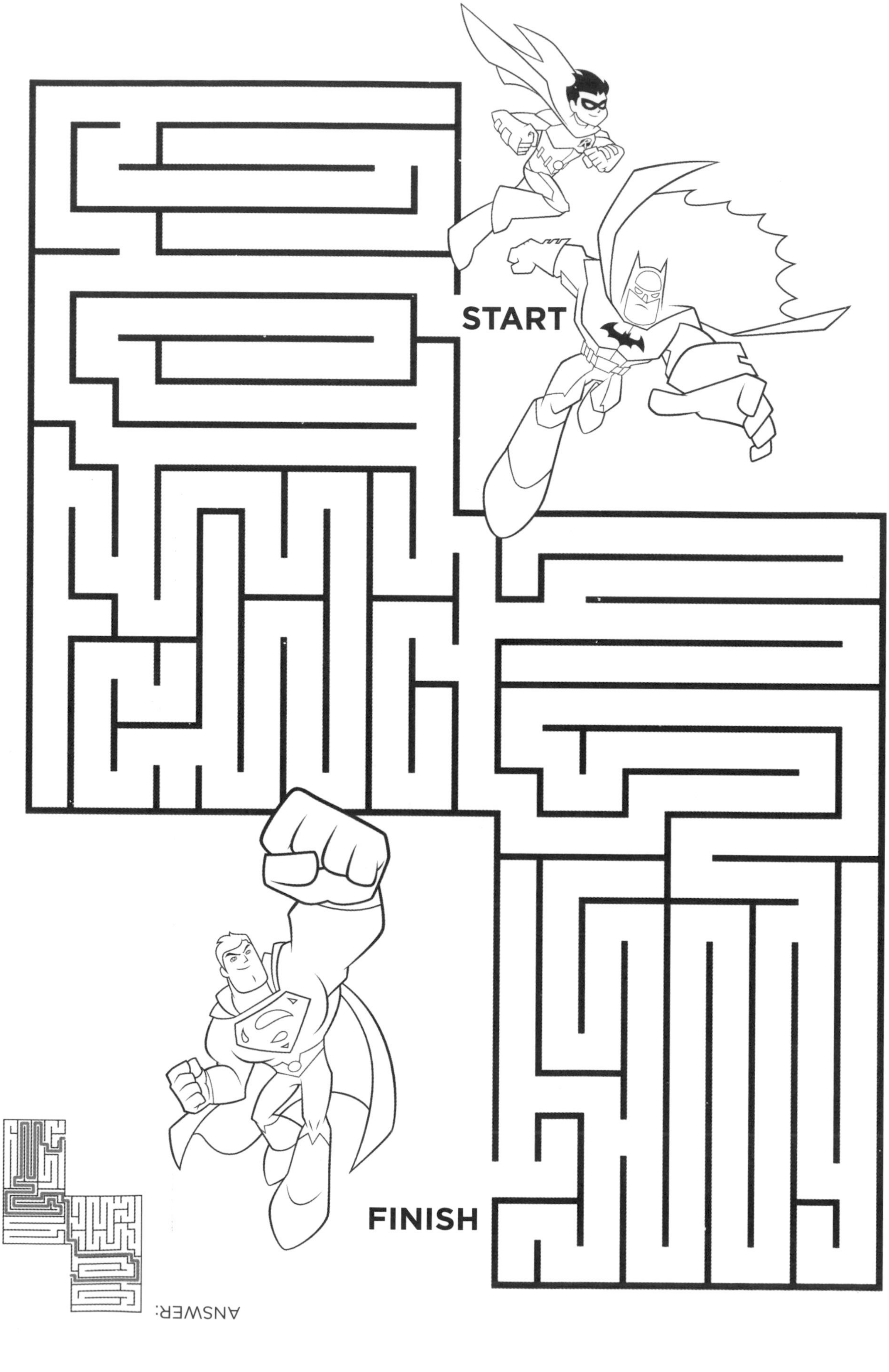
START
FINISH

ANSWER:

Use the grid to draw a picture of Batman.

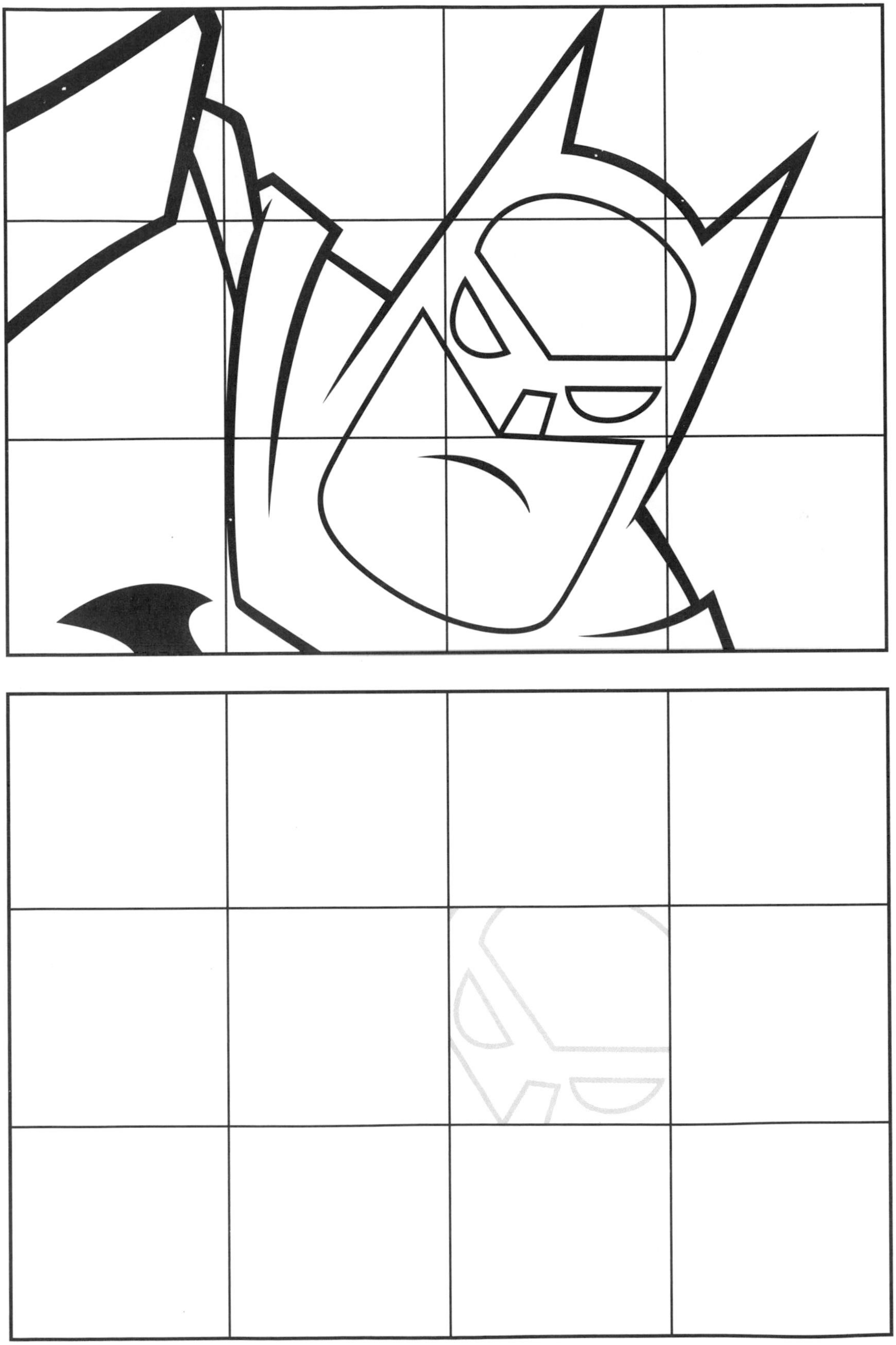

The Joker is one of Batman's greatest enemies!

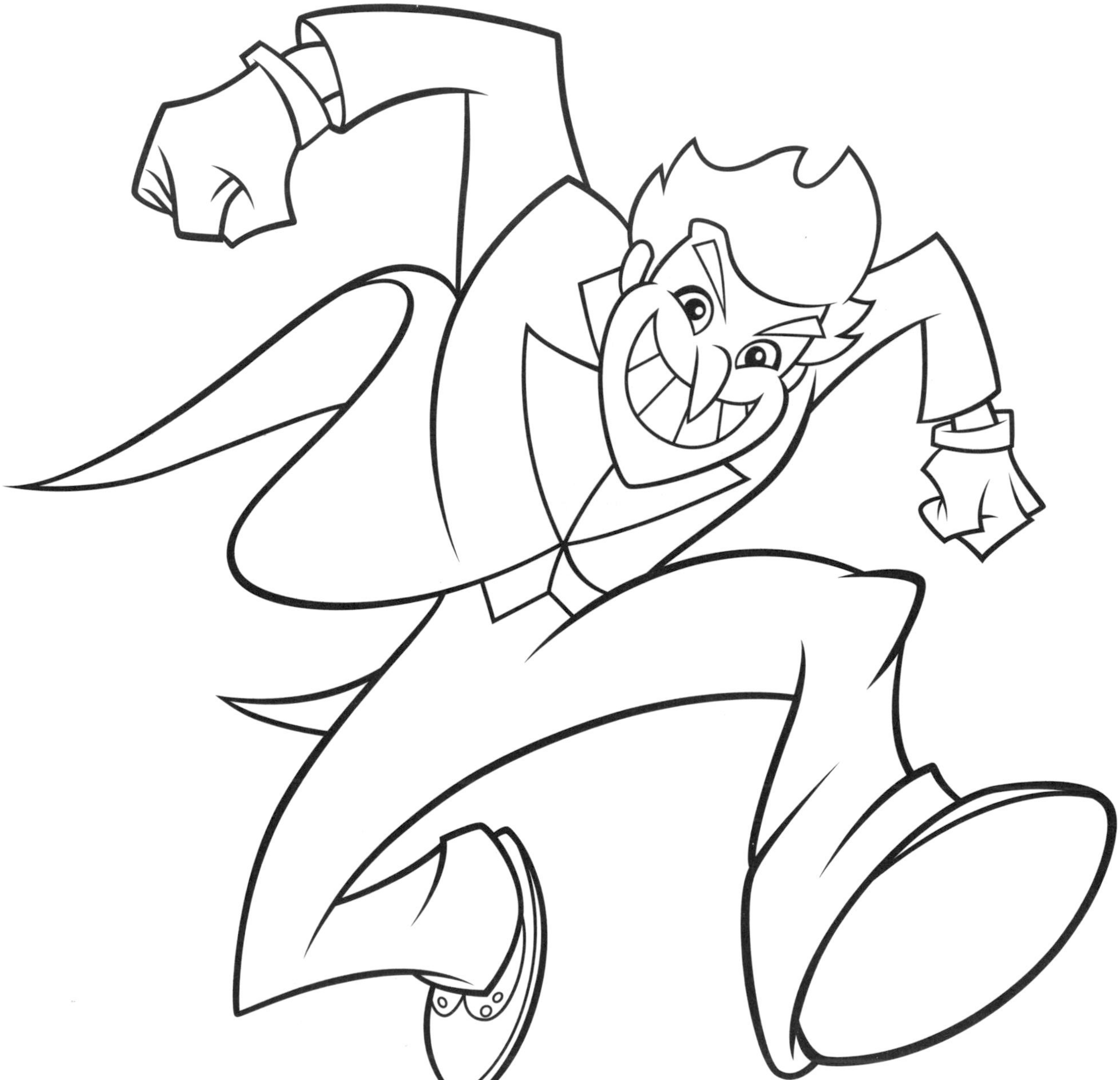

To learn the Joker's nickname, start at the arrow and, going clockwise around the circle, write the letters in order on the blanks.

___ ___ ___   ___ ___ ___ ___ ___

___ ___ ___ ___ ___ ___

___ ___   ___ ___ ___ ___ ___

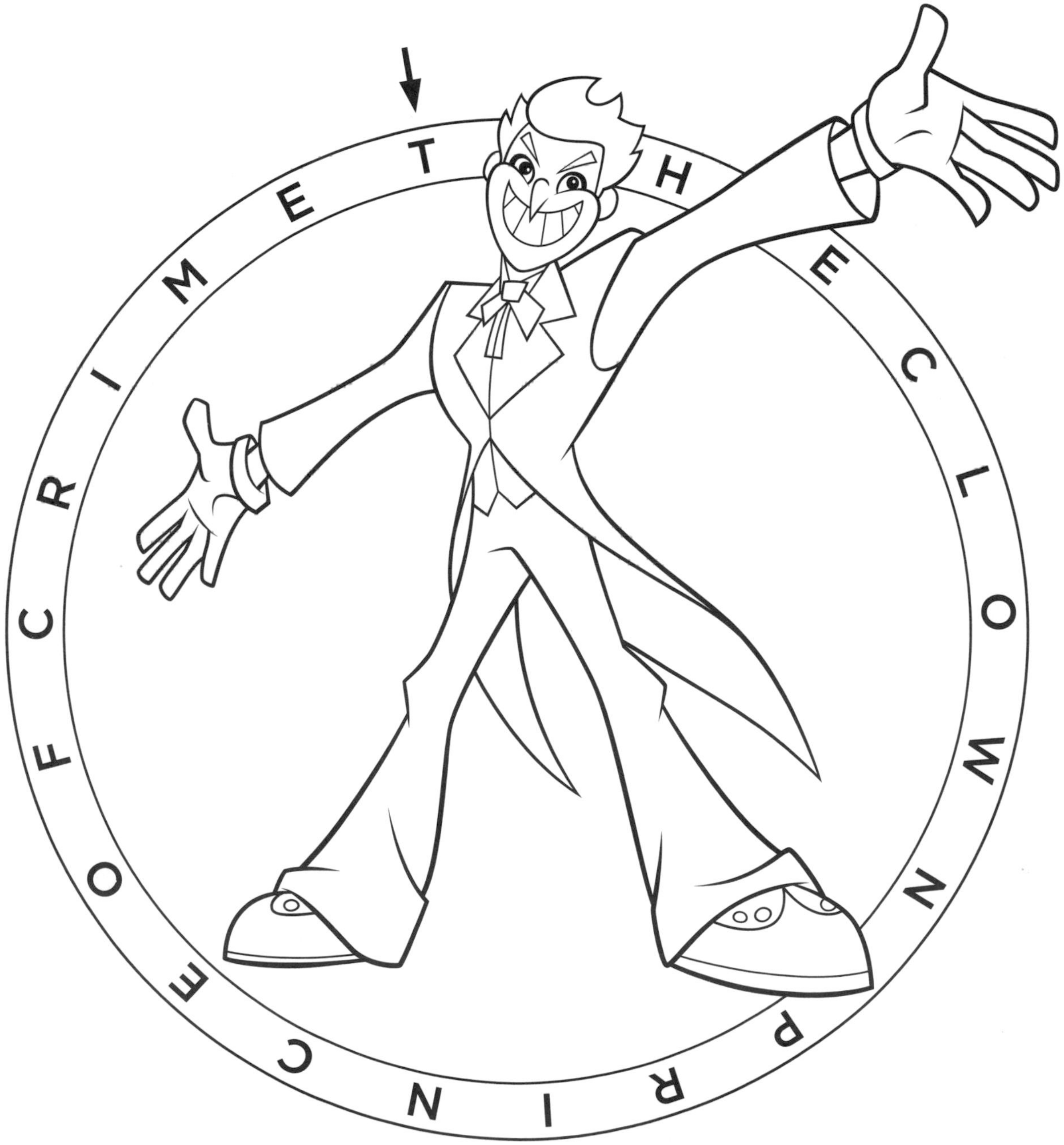
T H E C L O W N P R I N C E O F C R I M E

ANSWER: The Clown Prince of Crime.

Batman vs. the Joker!

With a friend, take turns connecting two dots with a straight line. If the line you draw completes a box, give yourself a point. If your box has the Joker in it, give yourself two points. If your box has Batman in it, give yourself three points. When no more boxes can be made, the player with more points wins.

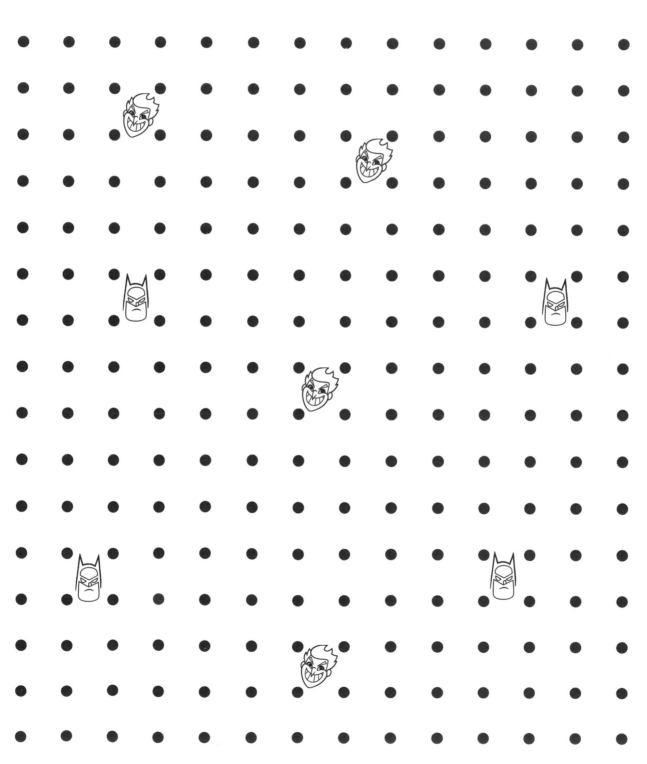

Play again!

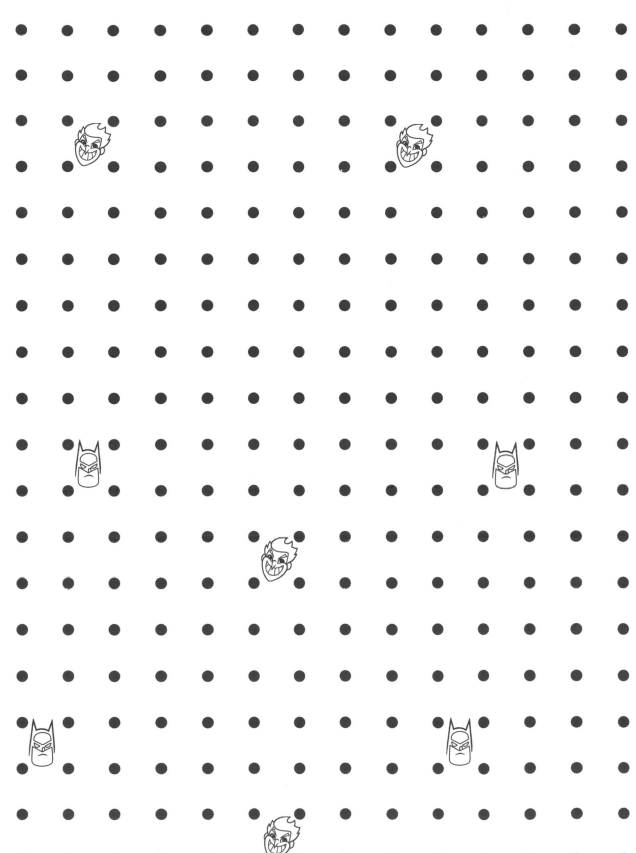

The Flash is the Fastest Man Alive! To find his nickname, cross out all the *Z*s. Write the remaining letters in order on the blanks.

Z T Z H E Z Z Z S Z C Z Z Z A Z R Z Z Z L Z E Z
T Z Z Z S Z P E Z E Z D Z S T Z Z Z E Z R

___ ___ ___   ___ ___ ___ ___ ___ ___ ___

___ ___ ___ ___ ___ ___ ___ ___ ___

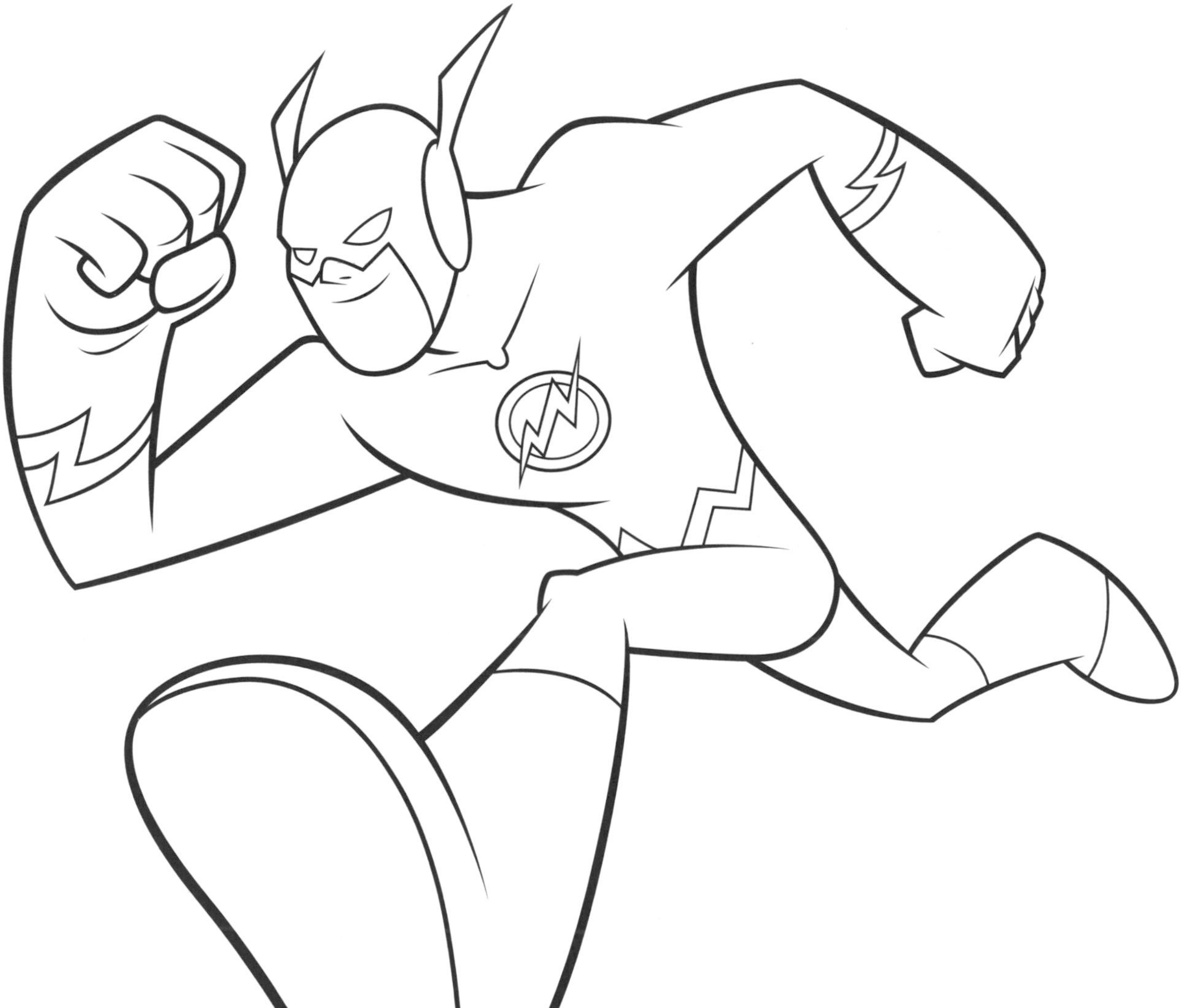

ANSWER: The Scarlet Speedster.

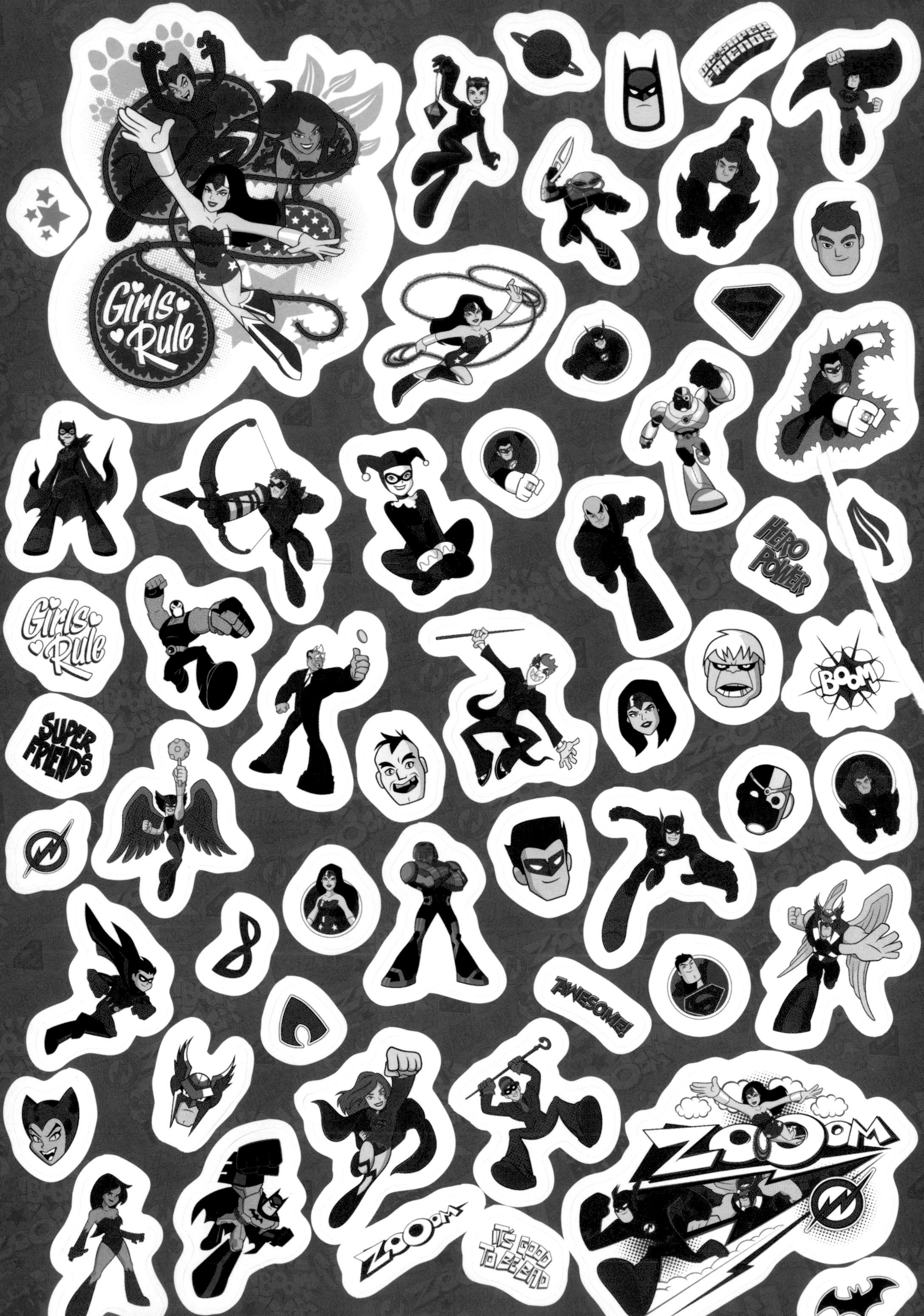
Girls Rule
HERO POWER
Girls Rule
SUPER FRIENDS
BOOM
AWESOME!
ZOOOM
ZOOOM
IT'S GOOD TO BE BAD

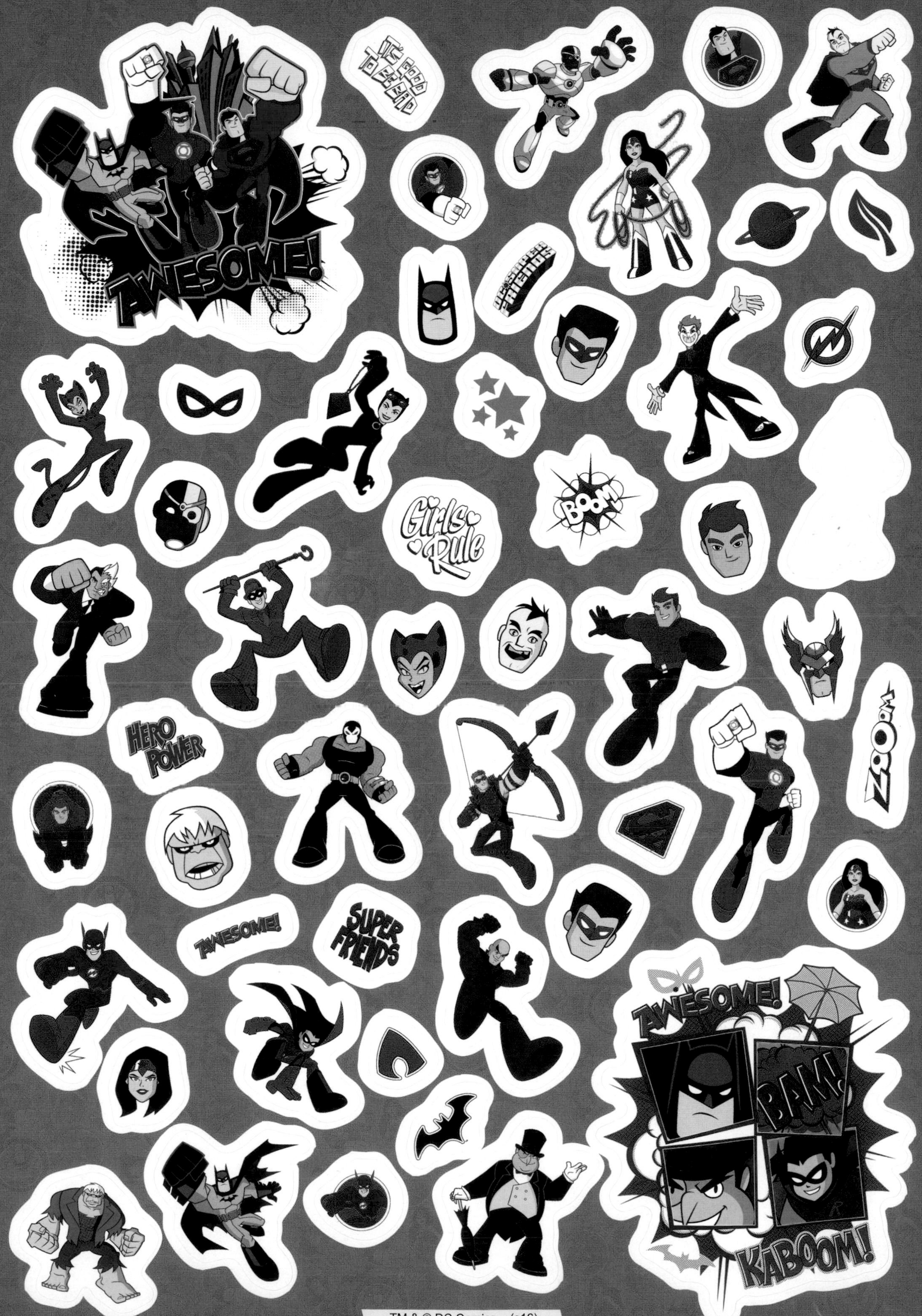
AWESOME!
Girls Rule
BOOM
HERO POWER
ZOOM
AWESOME!
SUPER FRIENDS
AWESOME!
BAM!
KABOOM!

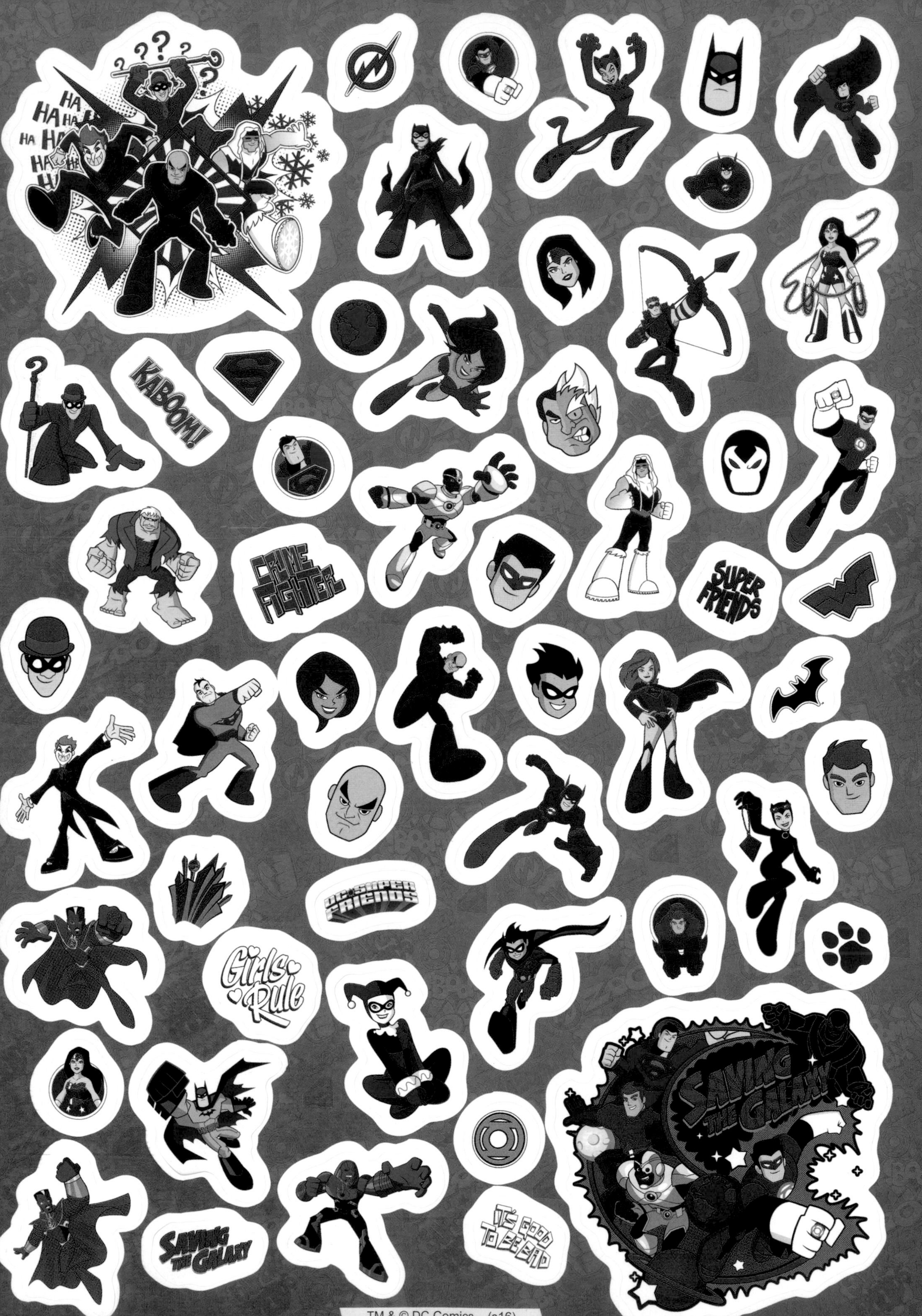

HA HA HA HA HA HA HA
KABOOM!
CRIME FIGHTER
SUPER FRIENDS
DC SUPER FRIENDS
Girls Rule
SAVING THE GALAXY
IT'S GOOD TO BE BAD
SAVING THE GALAXY

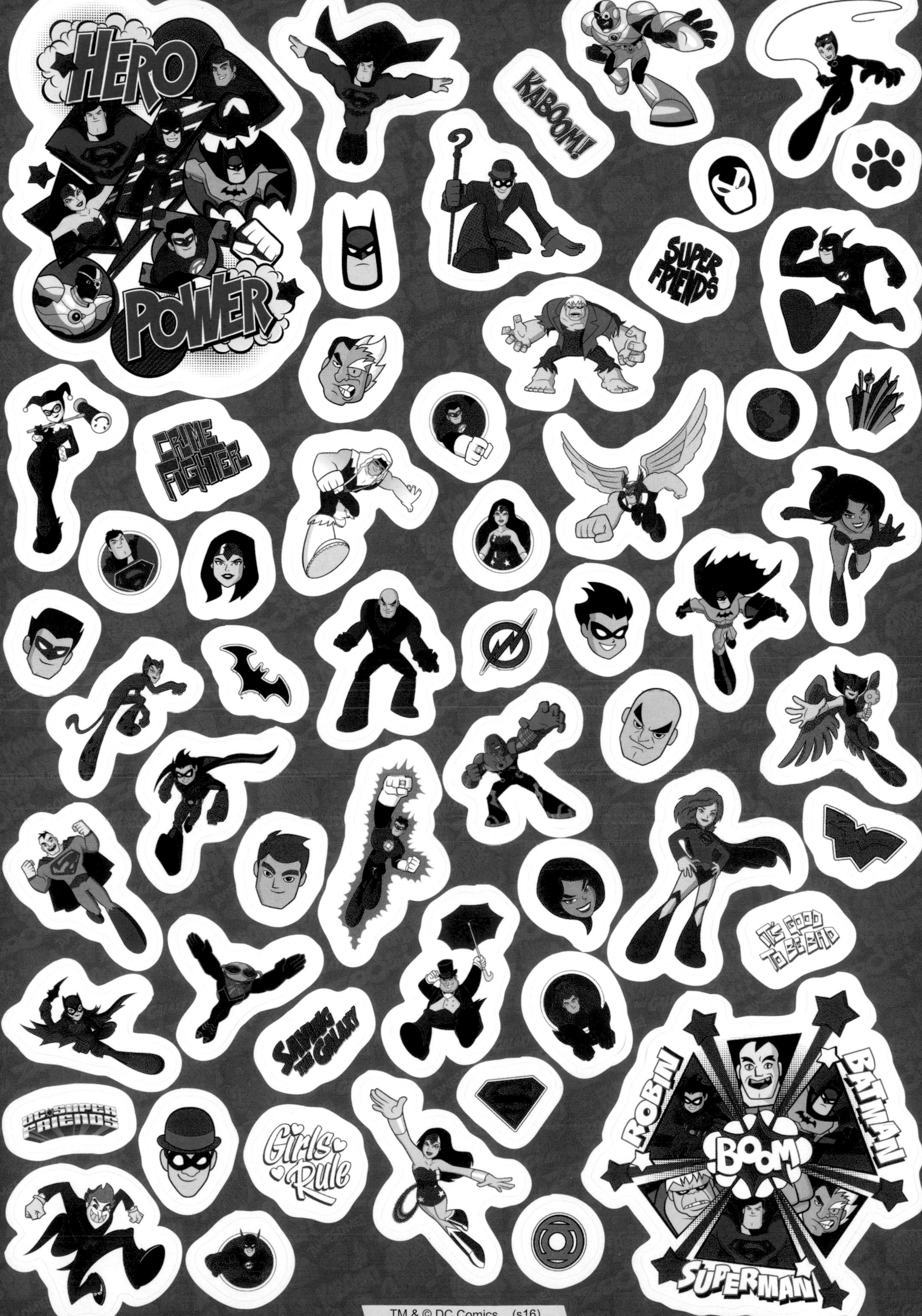
HERO
POWER
KABOOM!
SUPER FRIENDS
CRIME FIGHTER
DC SUPER FRIENDS
Girls Rule
ROBIN
BATMAN
BOOM!
SUPERMAN

To learn the name of this villain, circle every third letter. Then write those letters in order on the blanks.

A B C D E A F G P H I T J K A L M I
N O N P Q C R S O T U L V W D

___ ___ ___ ___ ___ ___ ___

___ ___ ___ ___

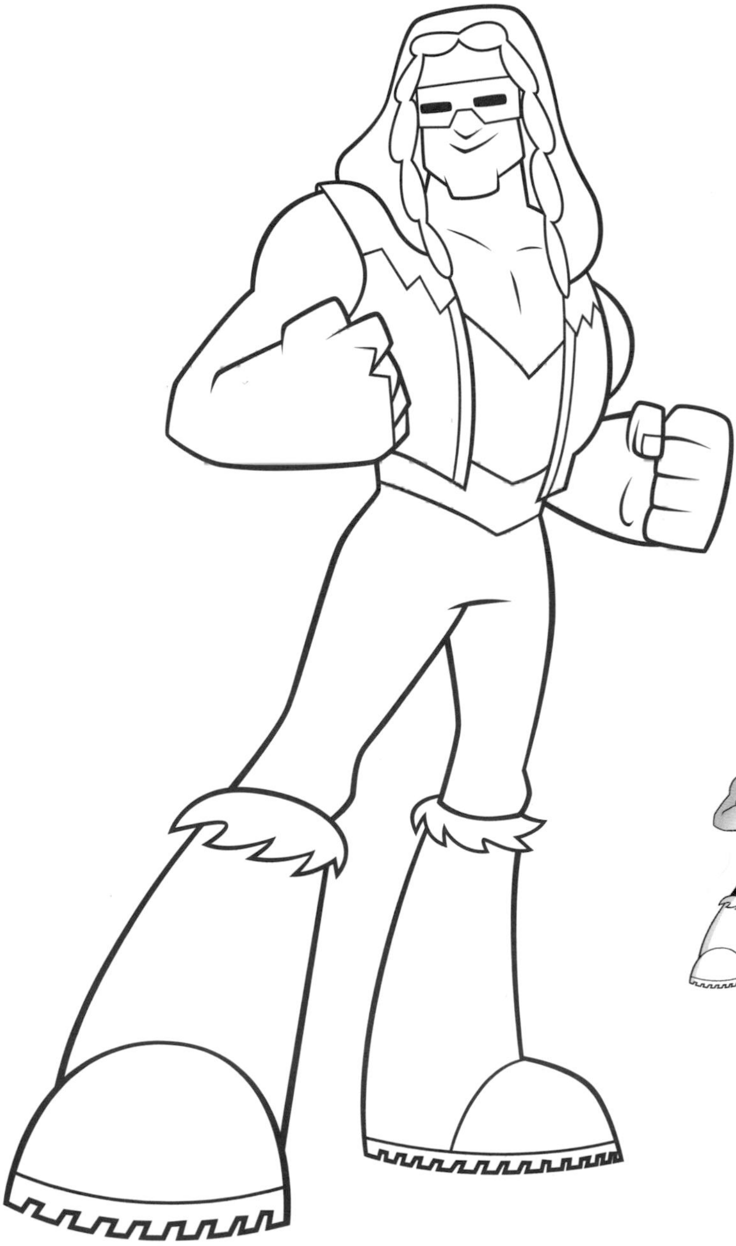

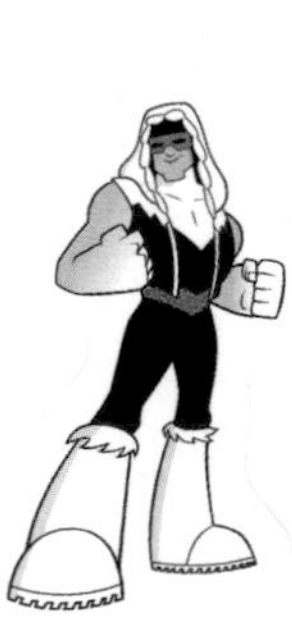

ANSWER: Captain Cold.

Help The Flash stop Captain Cold by solving the maze.

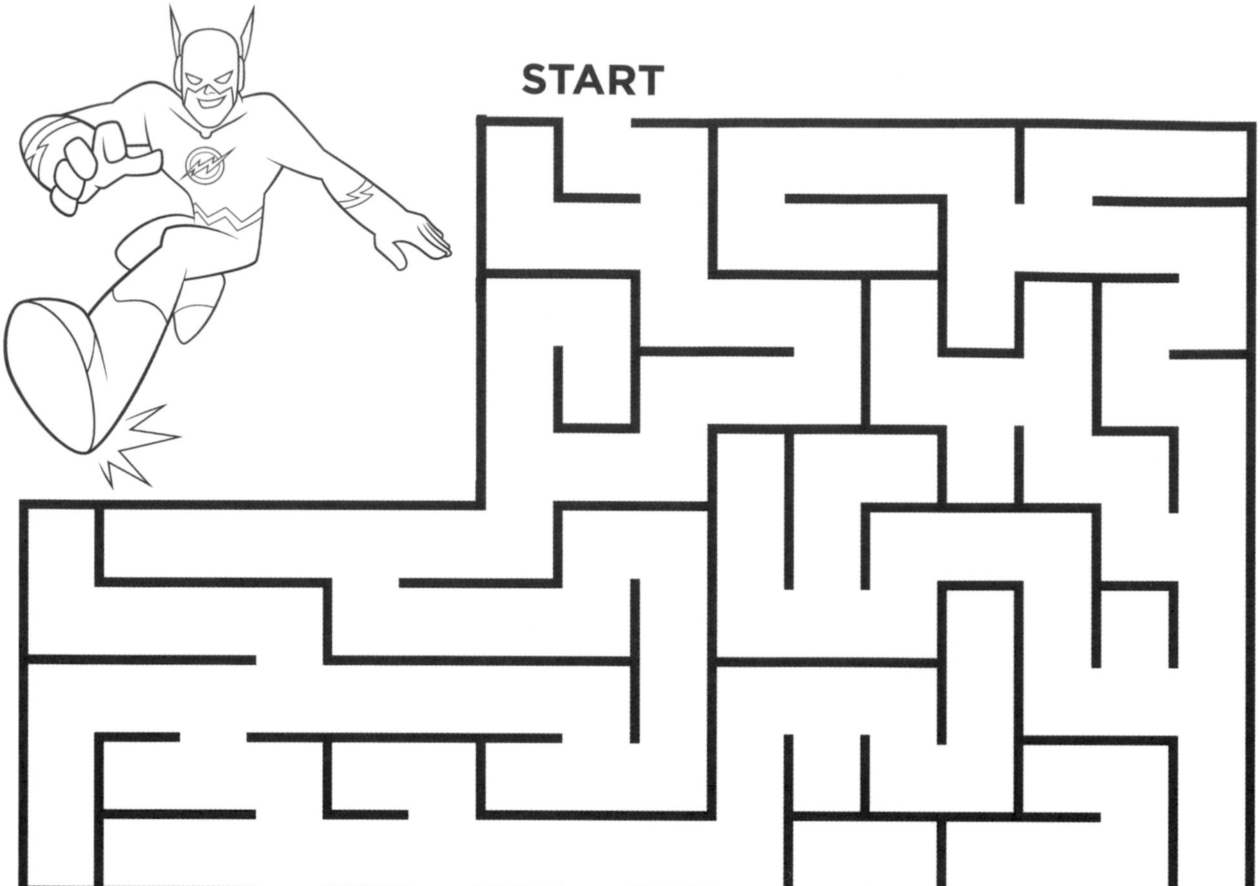

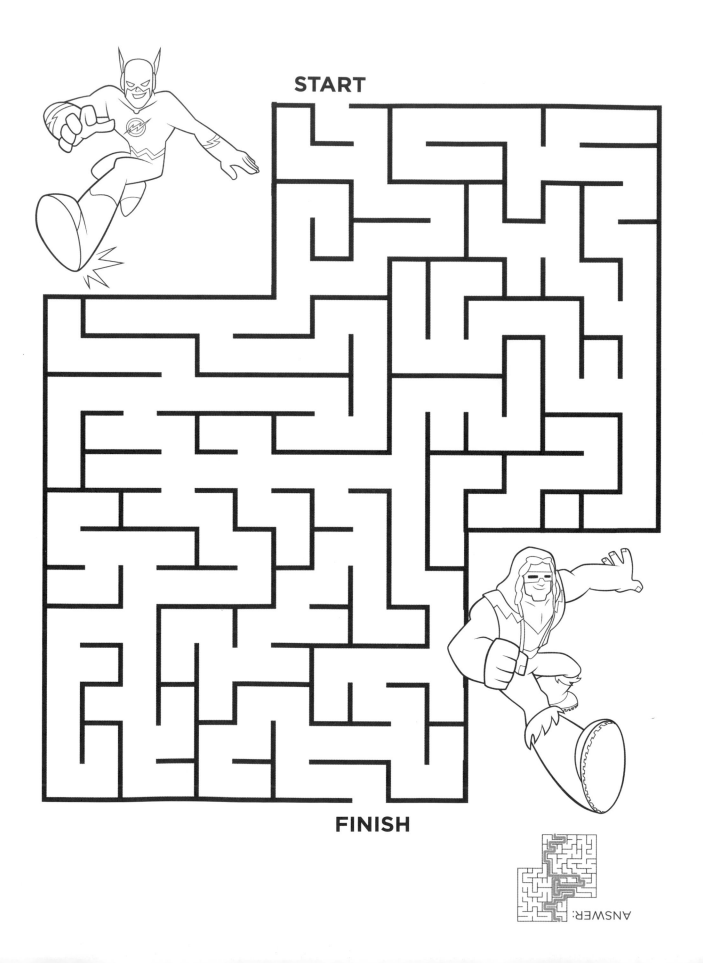

START
FINISH

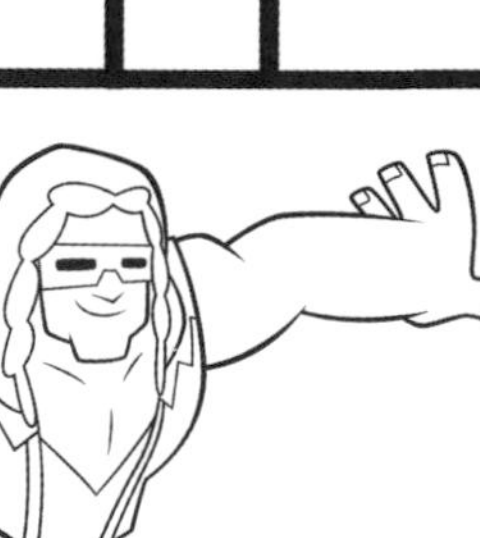

ANSWER:

Hawkman is heroic! Which two pictures of Hawkman are exactly the same?

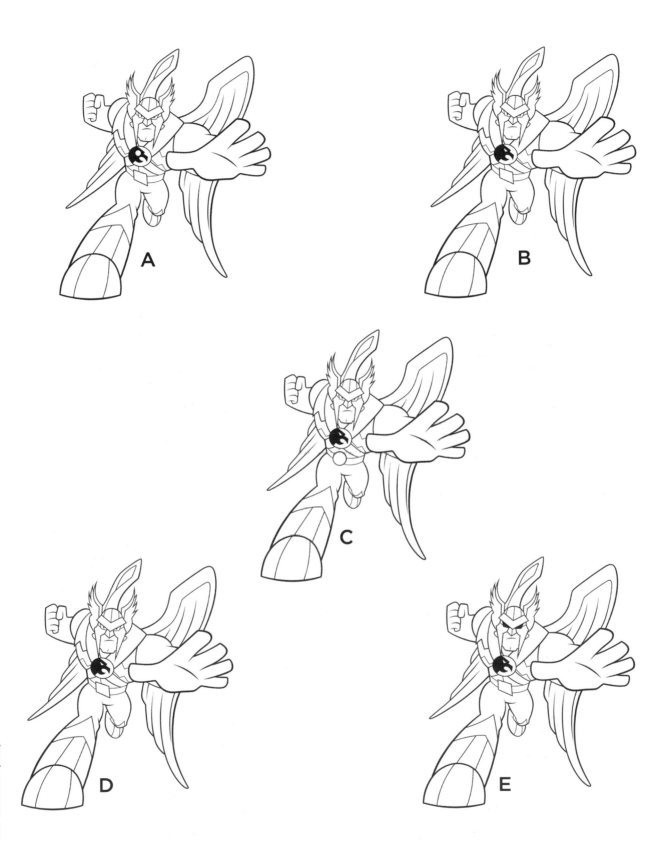

A

B

C

D

E

ANSWER: B and D.

Circle the shadow that belongs to Captain Cold.

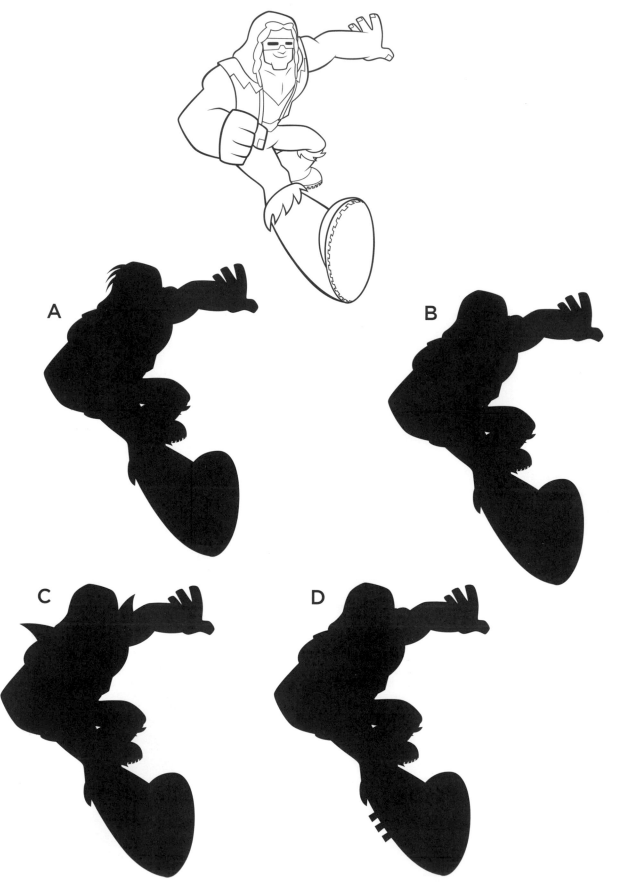

How many times can you find BANE in the puzzle?
Look up, down, forward, and backward.

A	B	A	N	E
B	A	N	E	N
E	N	A	B	A
N	E	N	A	B

ANSWER: 6.

TM & © DC Comics. (s16)

Use the grid to draw a picture of Bane.

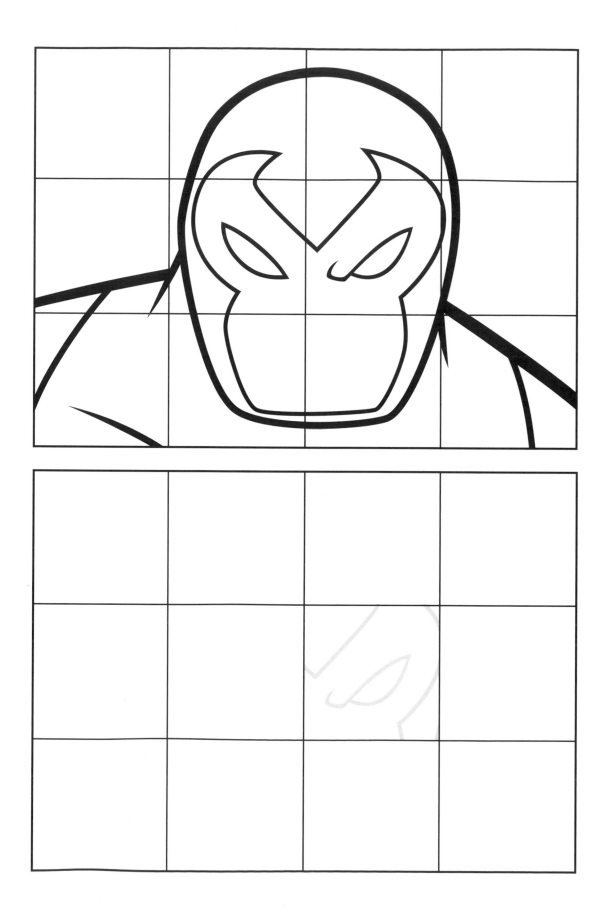

To learn the name of this deadly villain, replace each letter with the one that comes after it in the alphabet.

__ __ __ __ __ __ __ __ __

O N H R N M   H U X

ANSWER: Poison Ivy.

Circle the picture of Poison Ivy that is different from the others.

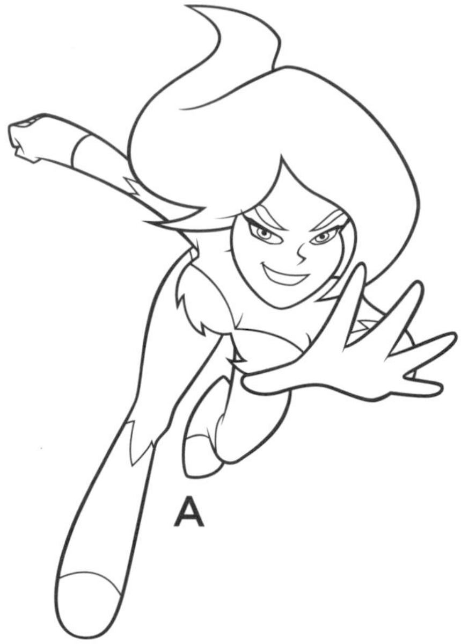

A

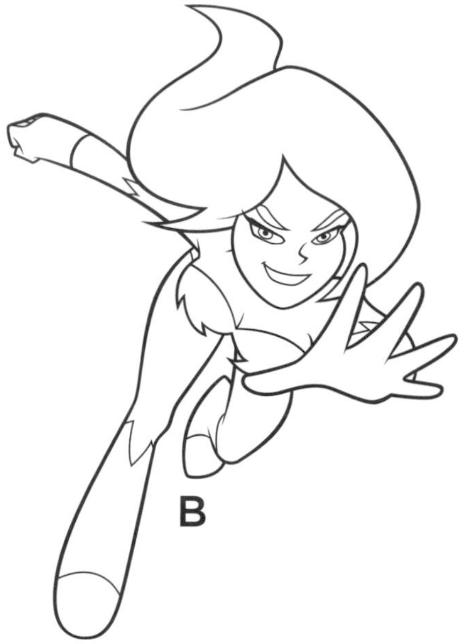

B

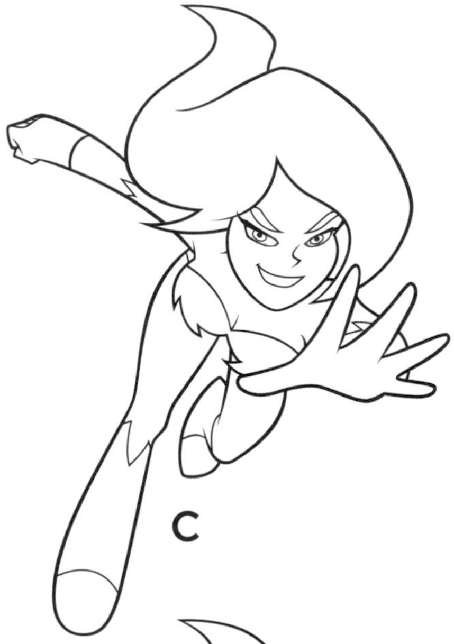

C

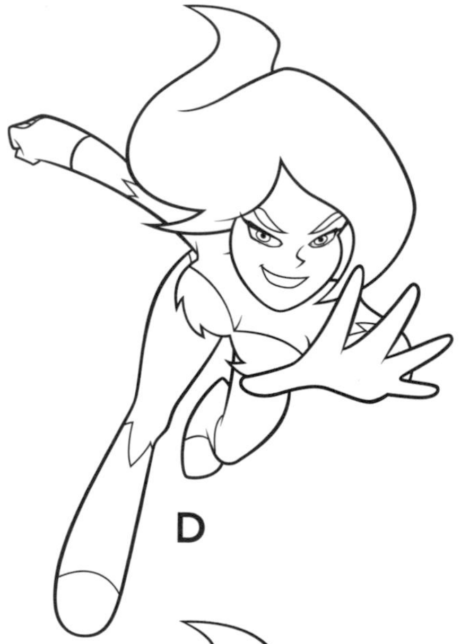

D

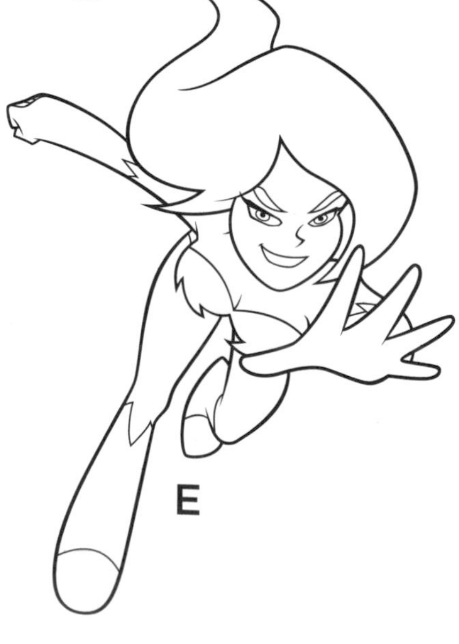

E

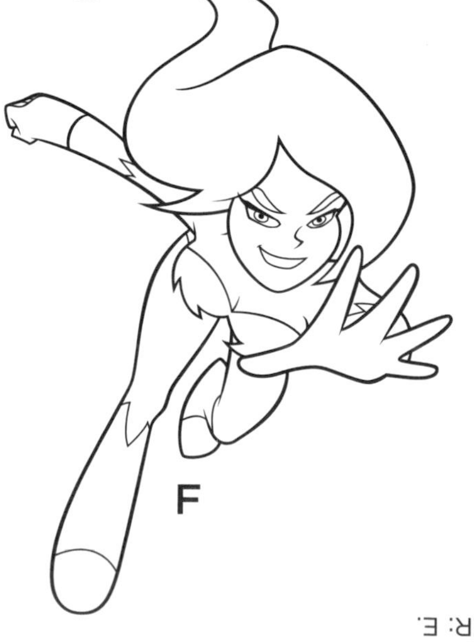

F

ANSWER: E.

Cross out all the pictures of the Cheetah and Poison Ivy.
How many pictures of Wonder Woman are left?

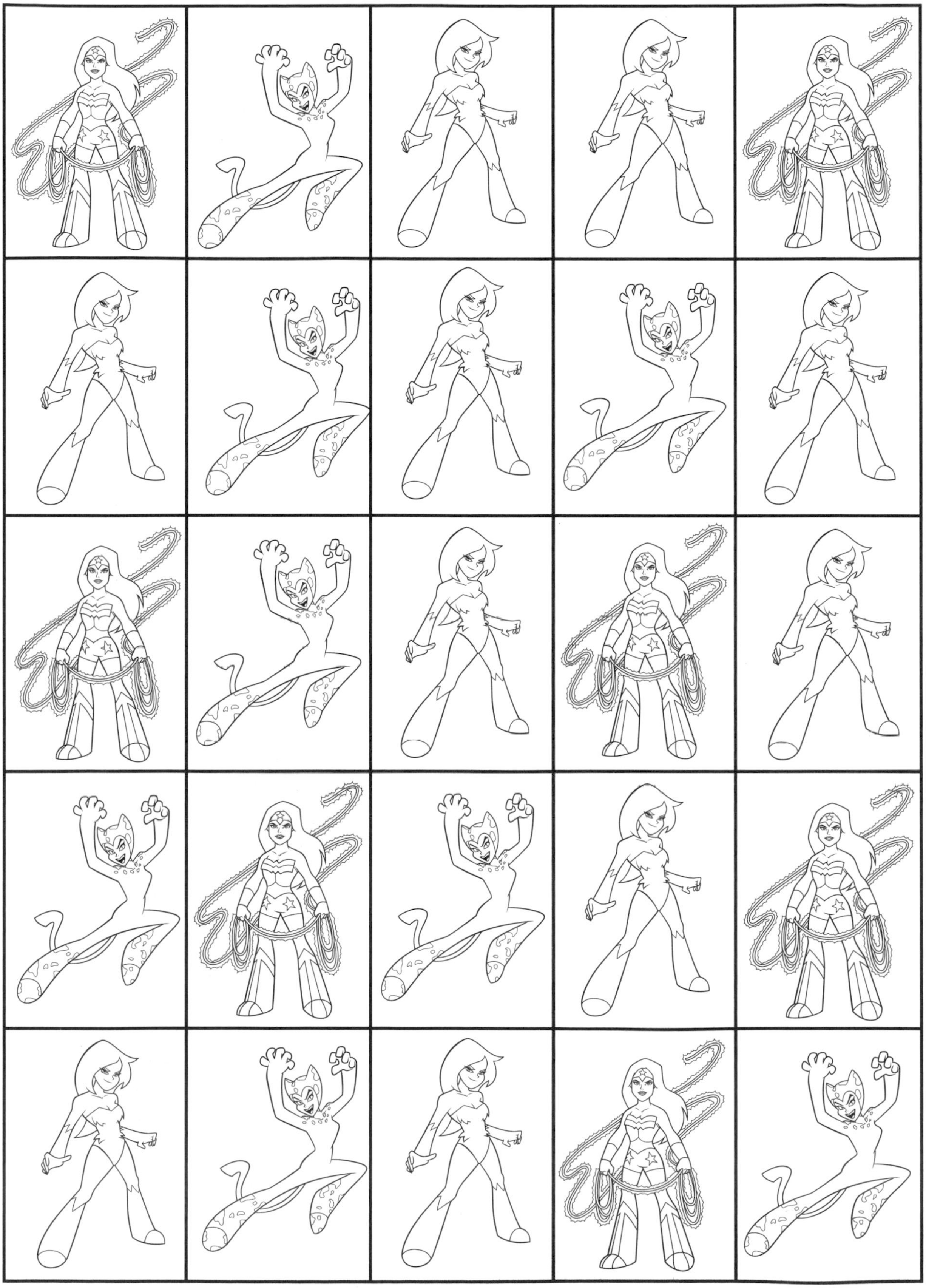

ANSWER: 7.

Draw a line from each hero to his shadow.

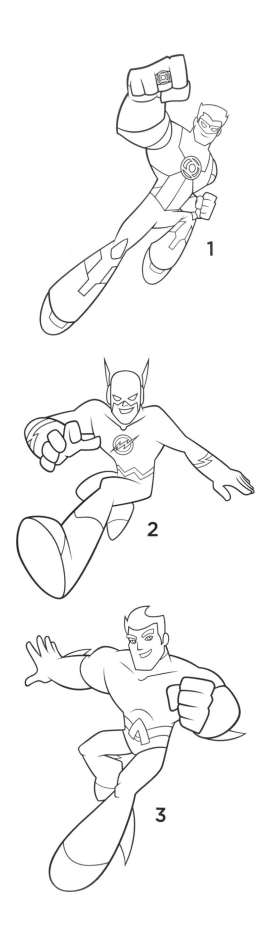

1

2

3

A

B

C

Help Wonder Woman find the path that leads to Poison Ivy.

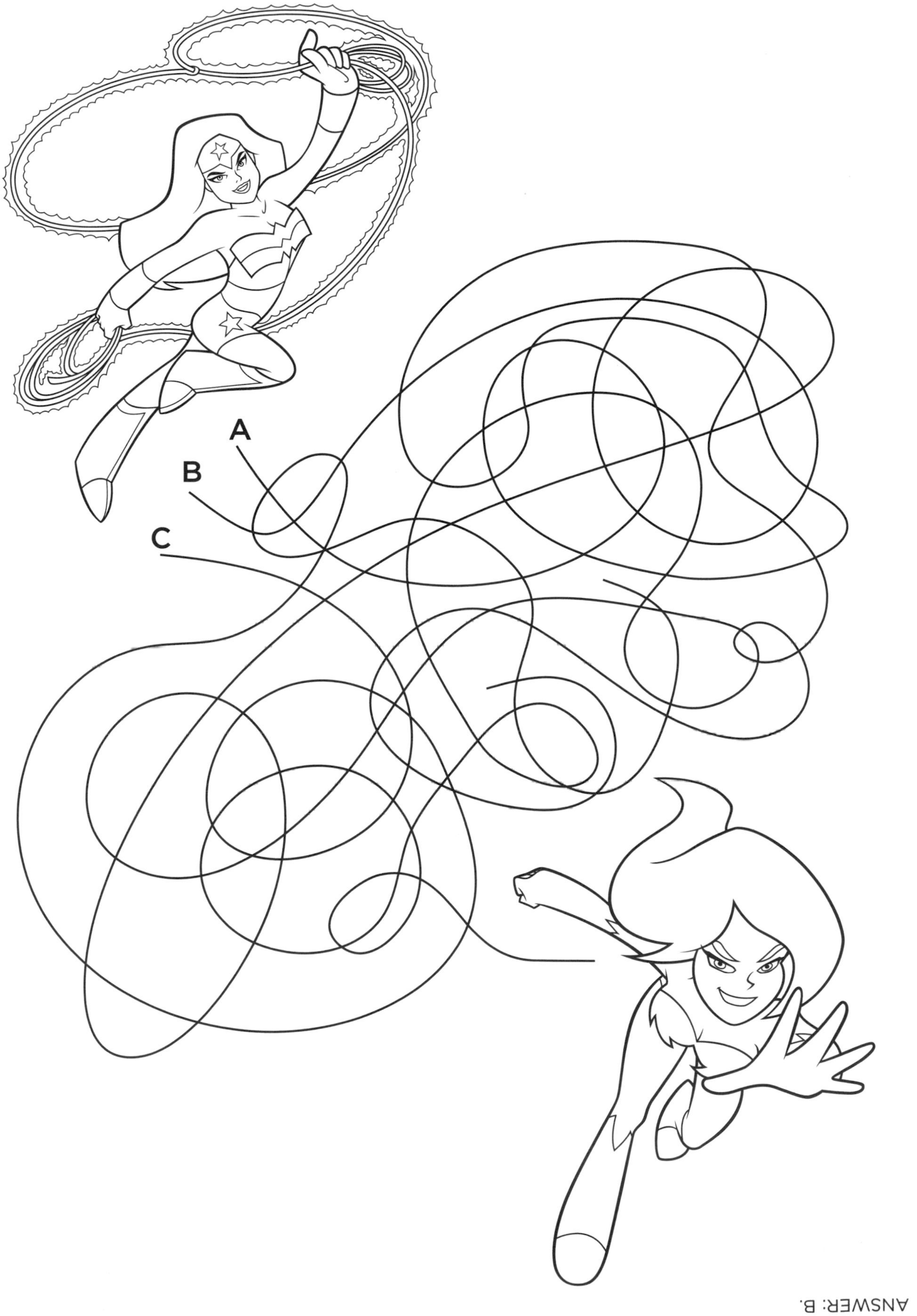
A
B
C

ANSWER: B.

Green Lantern can create almost anything with his power ring! Draw what you think Green Lantern is making now.

Draw a line from each picture to its close-up.

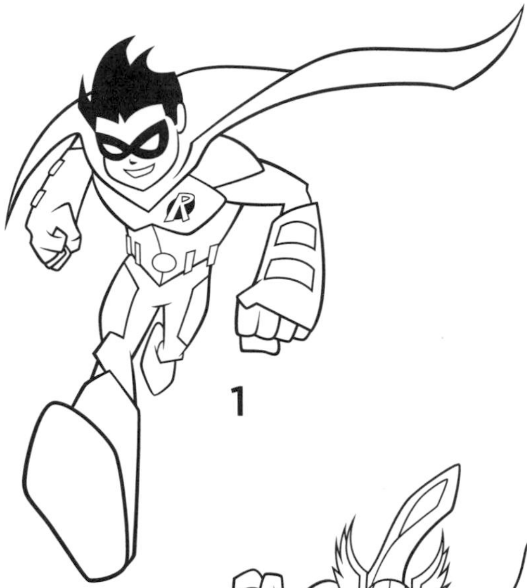

1

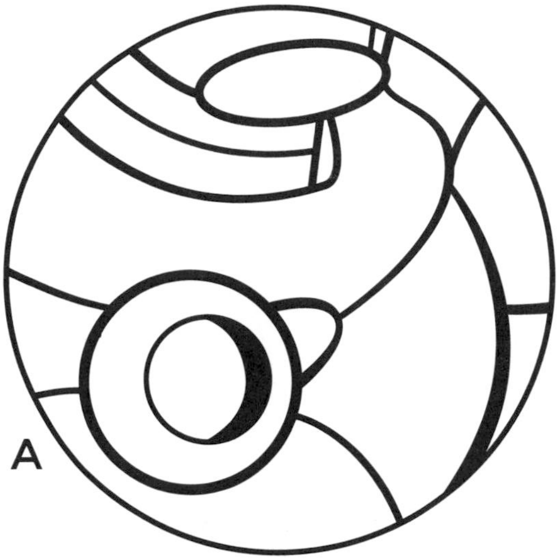

A

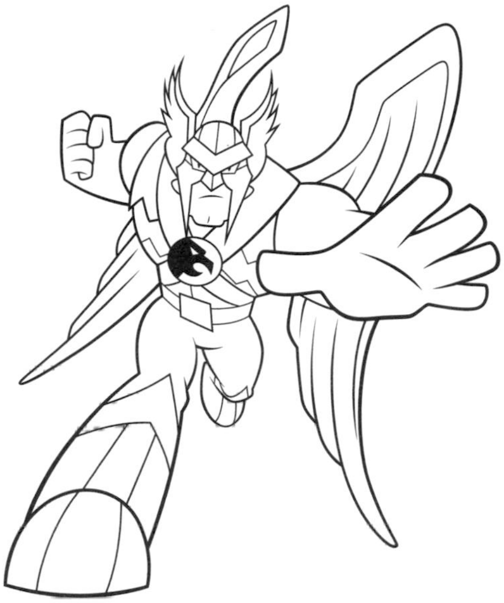

2

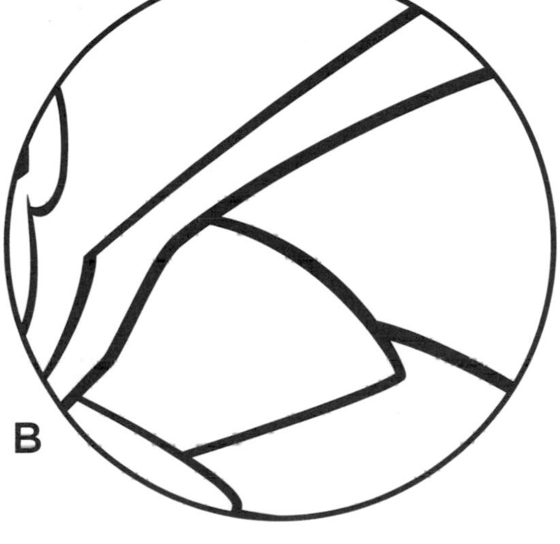

B

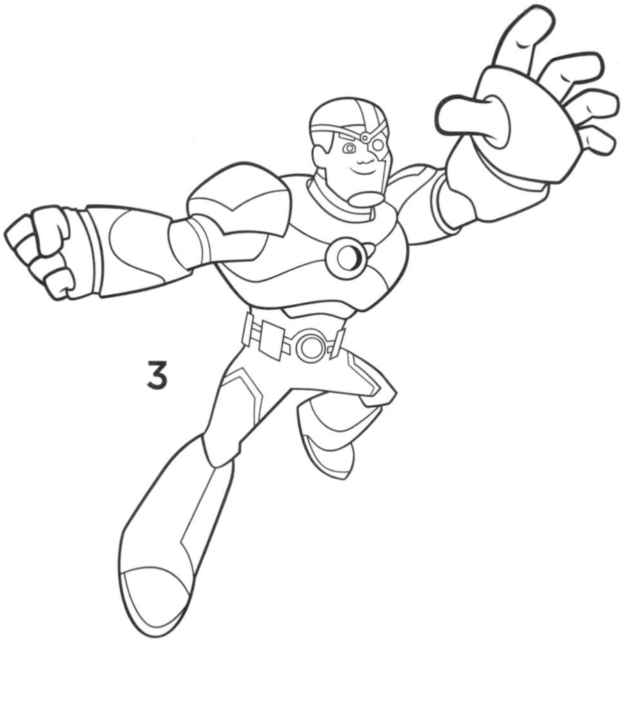

3

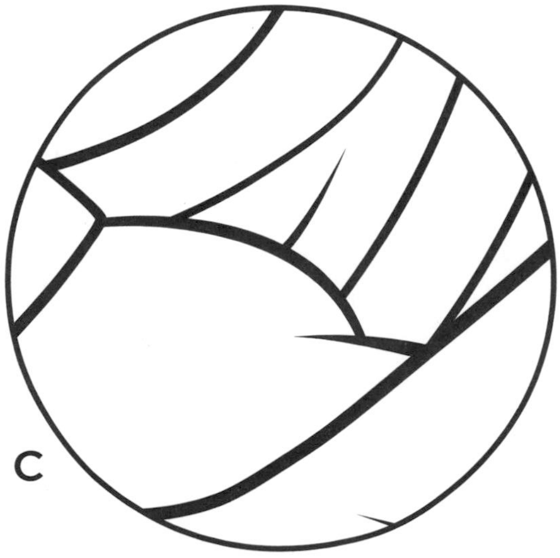

C

ANSWER: 1-B; 2-C; and 3-A.

Cyborg is a high-tech hero! Complete this picture of him. Use the smaller image as your guide.

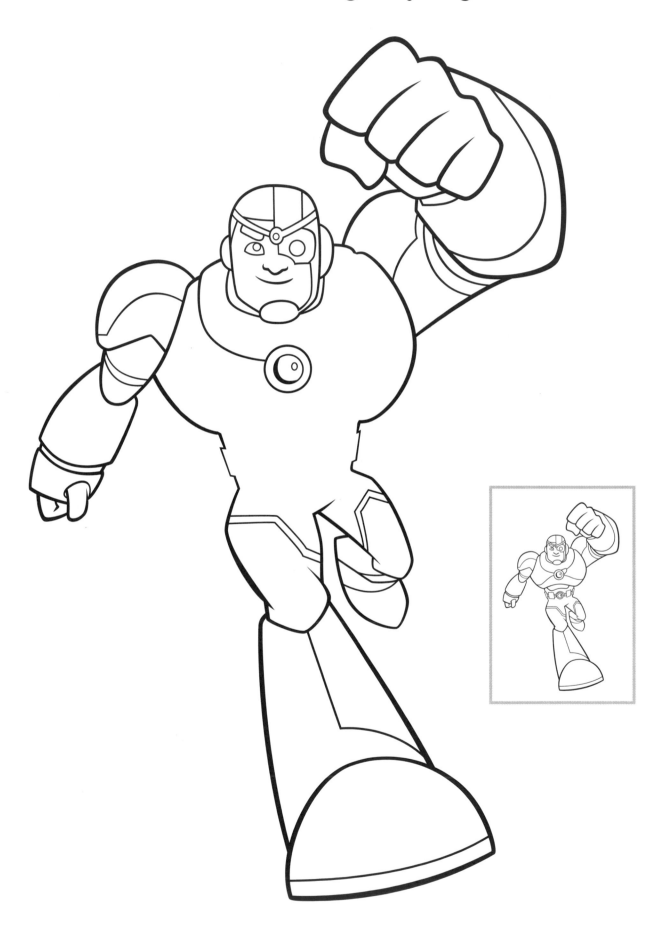

To learn the name of this tricky villain, replace each letter with the one that comes after it in the alphabet.

___ ___ ___   ___ ___ ___ ___ ___ ___ ___

S G D   Q H C C K D Q

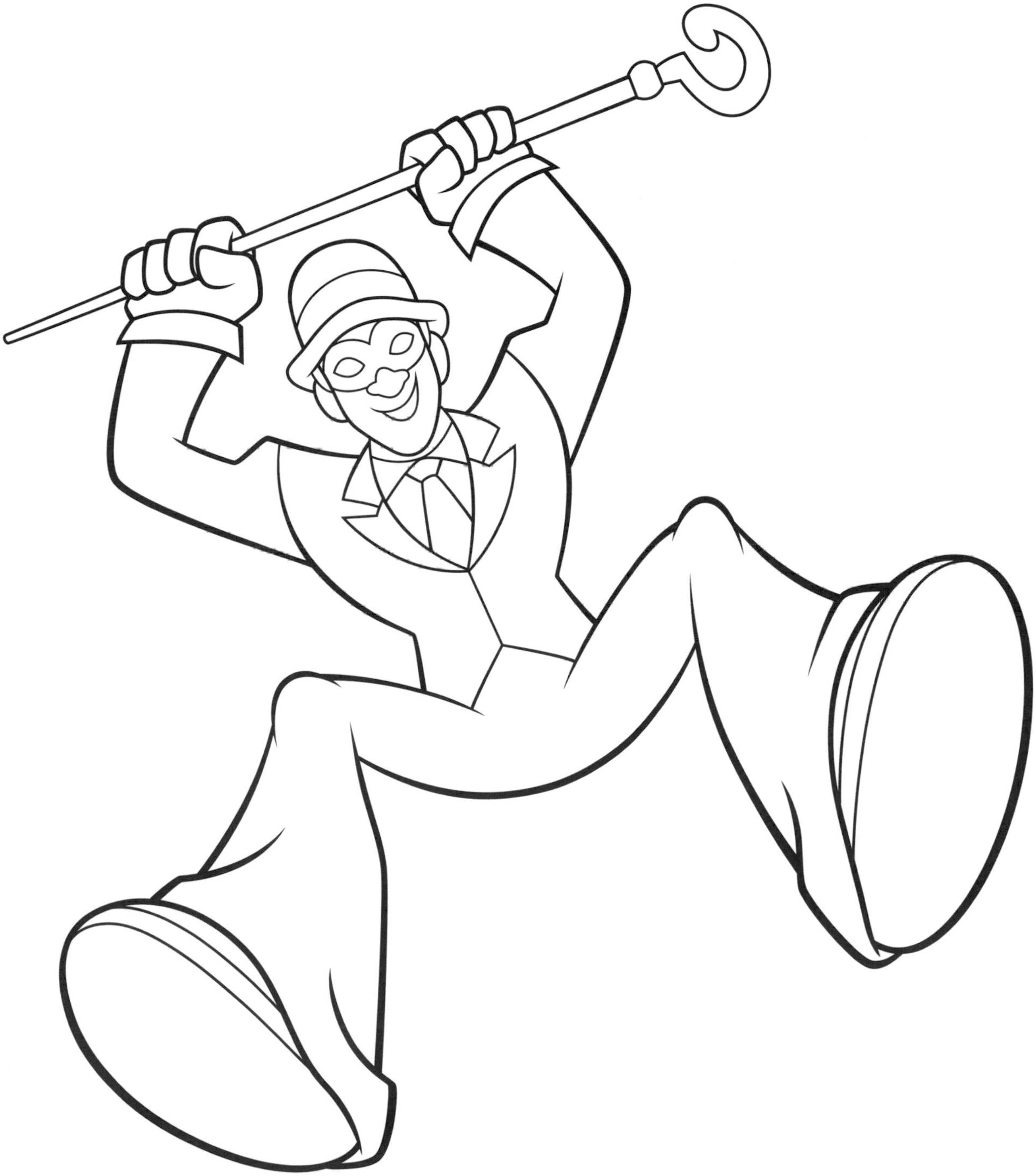

ANSWER: The Riddler.

Circle the image that is different in each row.

1

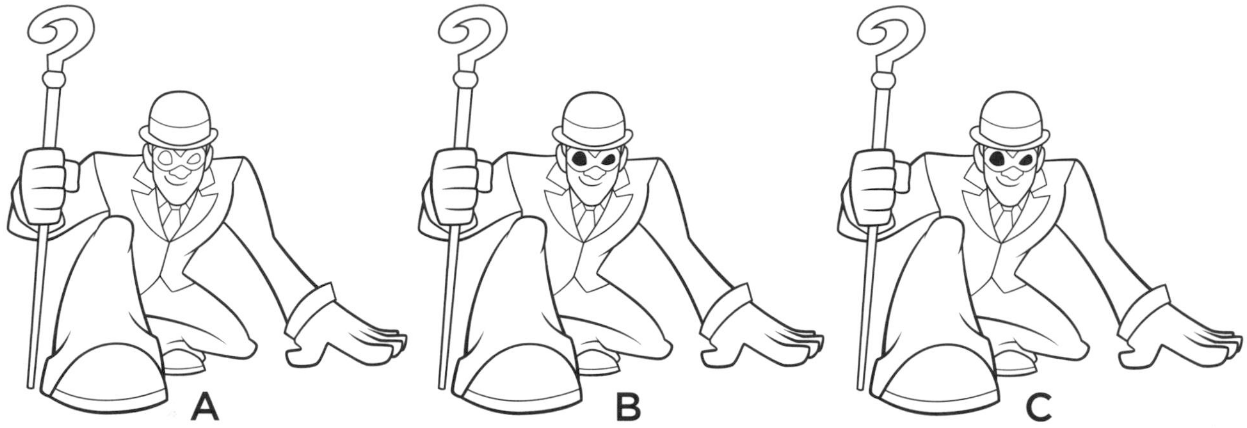

A B C

2

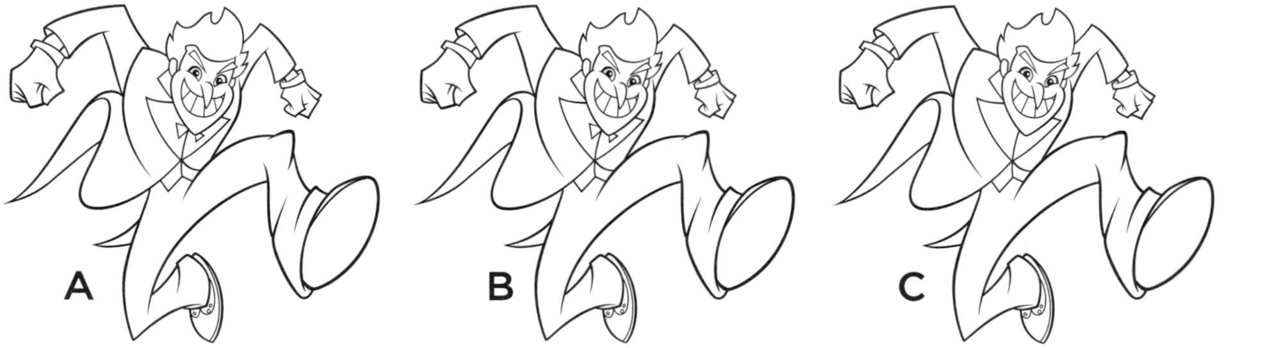

A B C

3

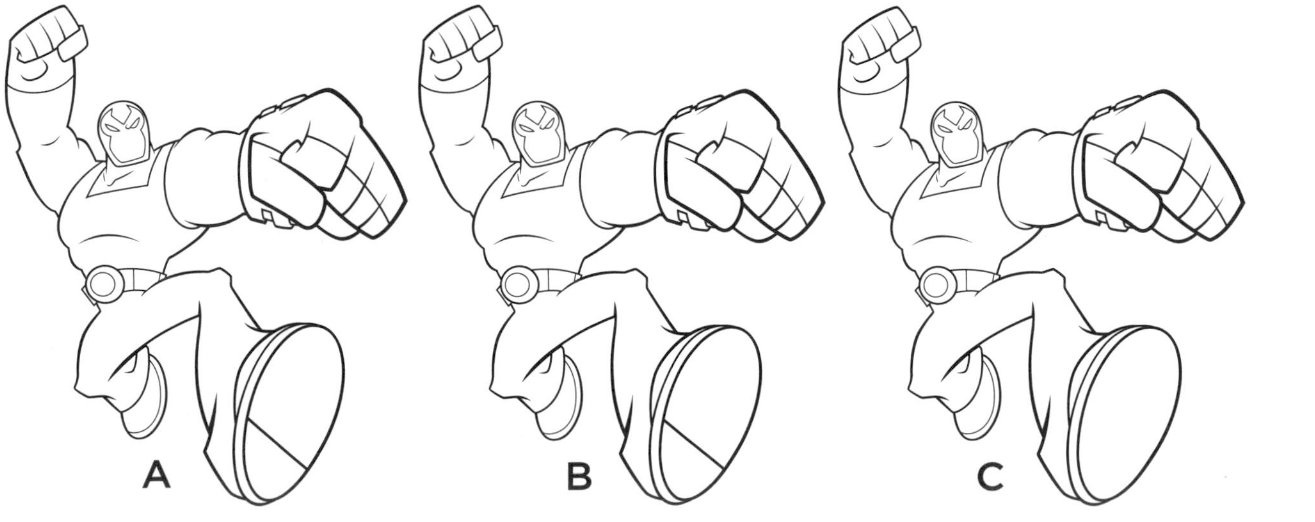

A B C

ANSWER: 1-A, 2-C; and 3-C.

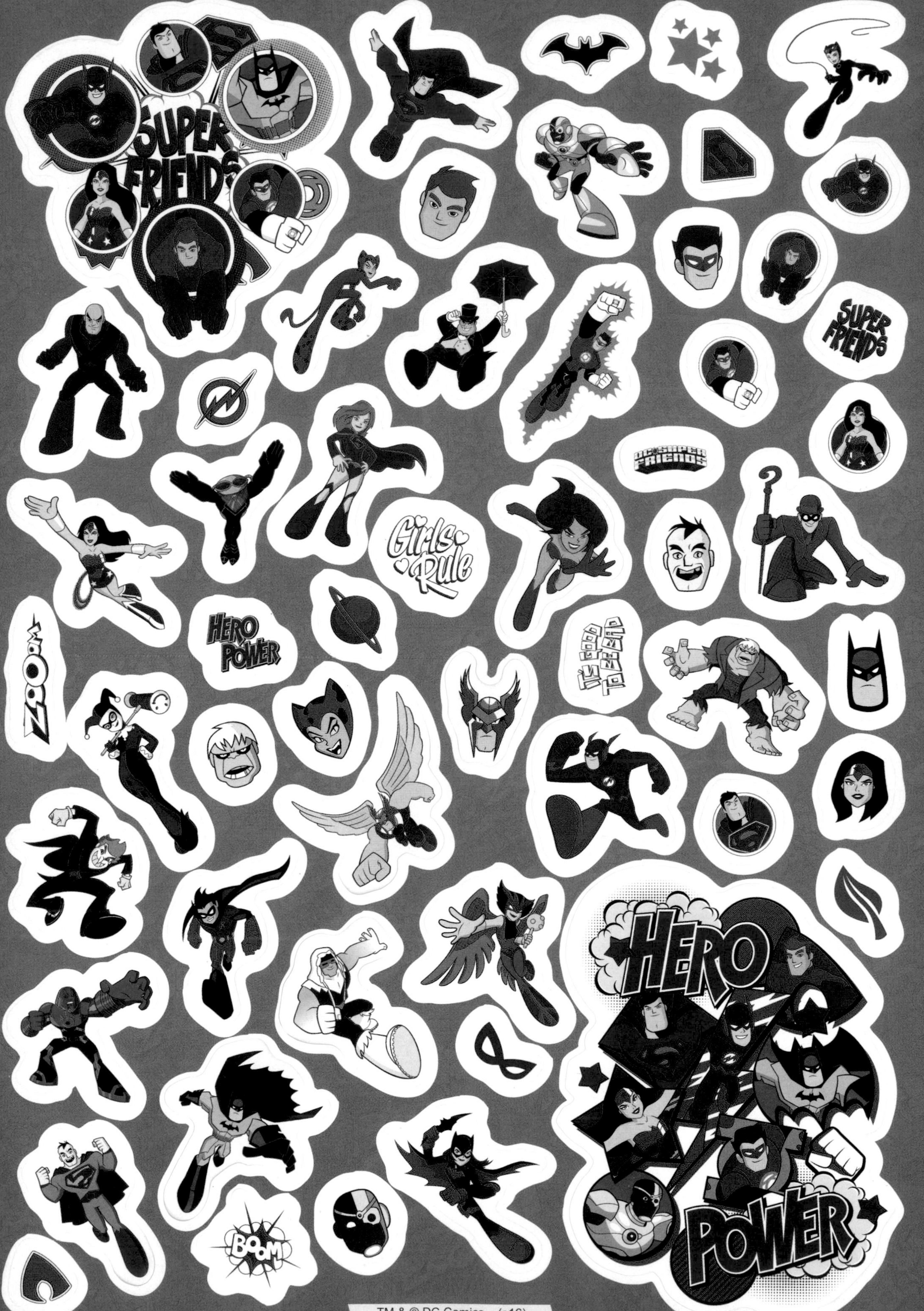

SUPER FRIENDS
SUPER FRIENDS
DC SUPER FRIENDS
Girls Rule
HERO POWER
IT'S GOOD TO BE GOOD
ZOOOM
HERO POWER
BOOM!

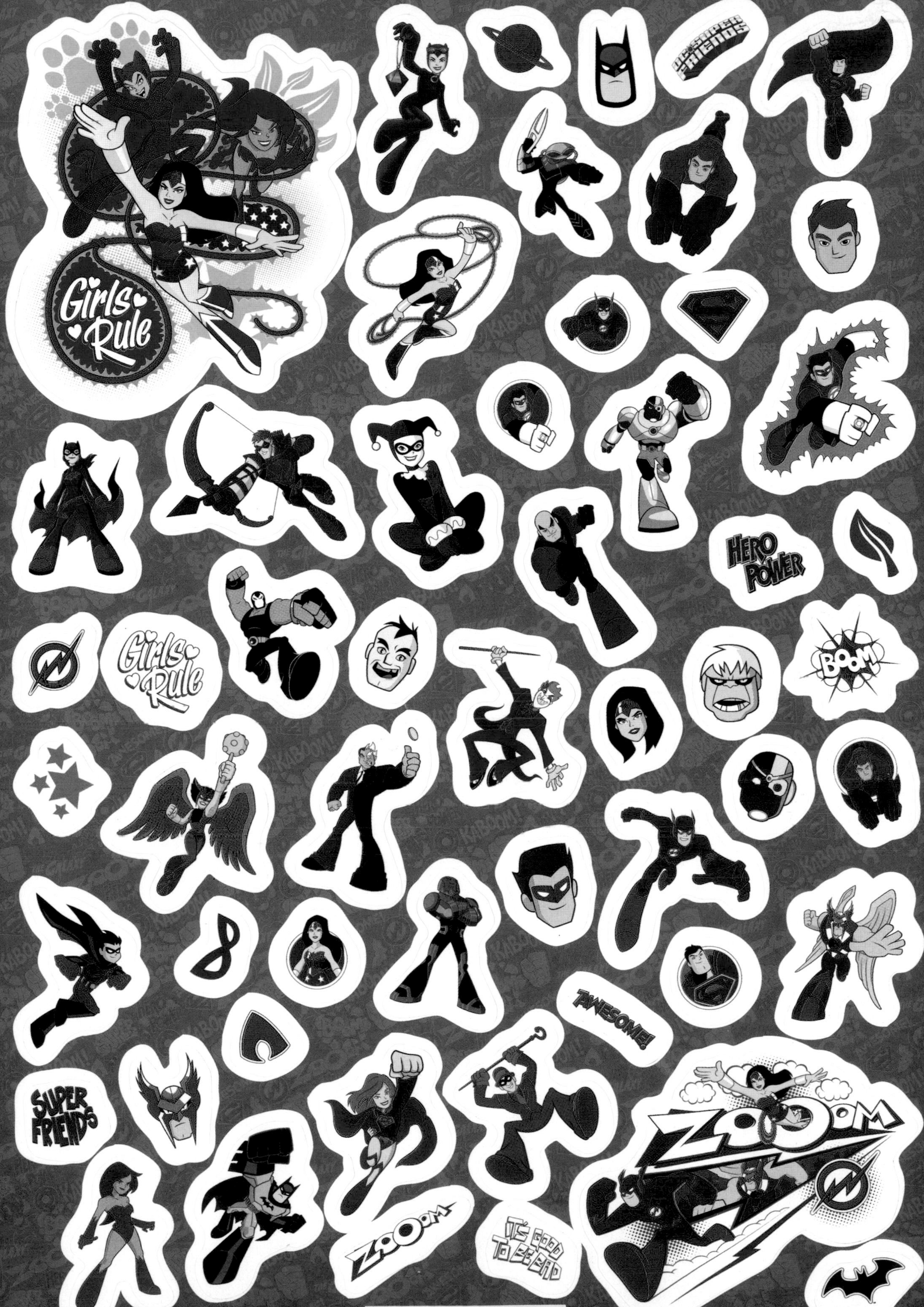
Girls Rule
DC SUPER FRIENDS
HERO POWER
Girls Rule
BOOM!
AWESOME!
SUPER FRIENDS
ZOOOM
ZOOOM
IT'S GOOD TO BE BAD

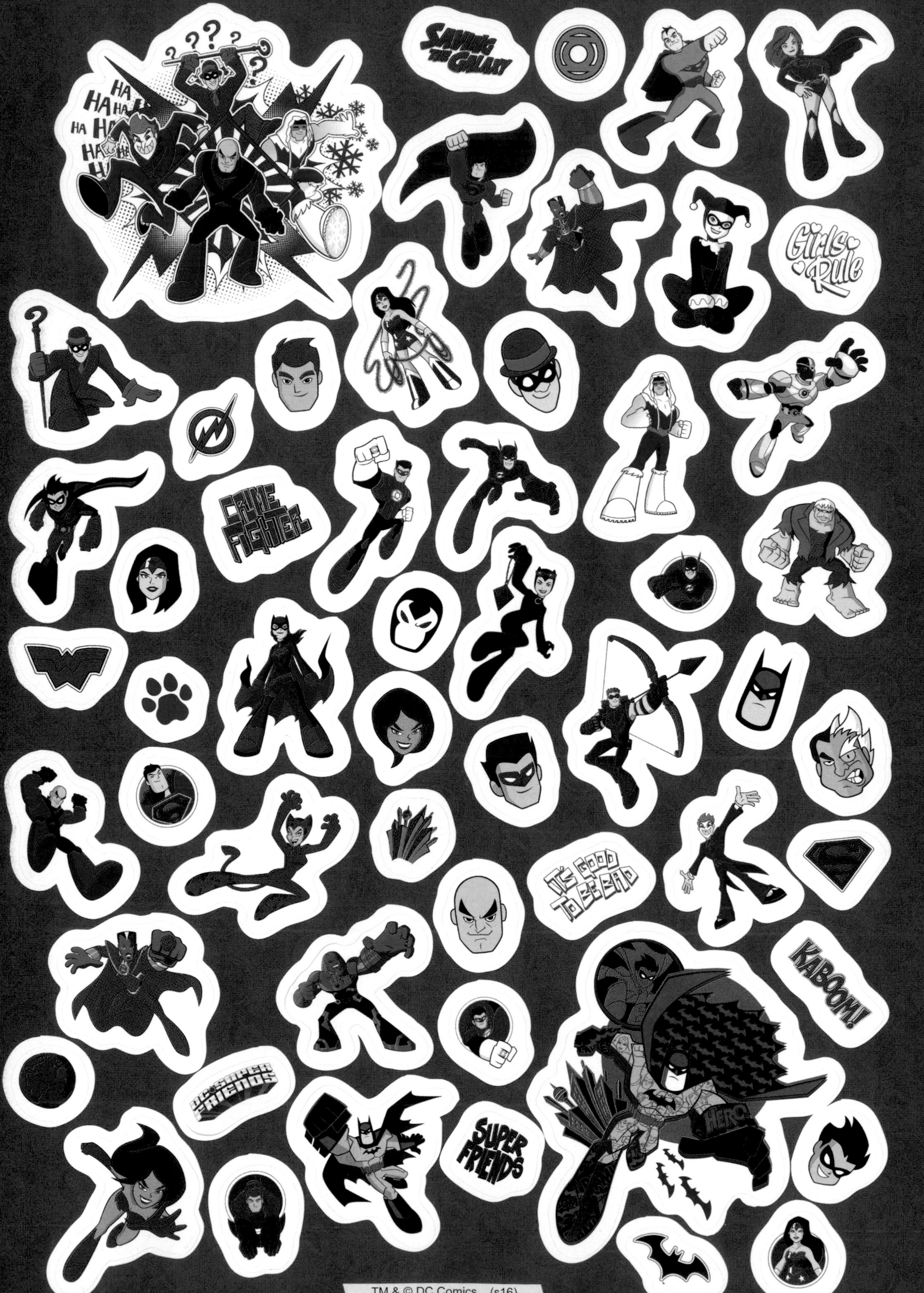
SAVING THE GALAXY
Girls Rule
CRIME FIGHTER
IT'S GOOD TO BE BAD
KABOOM!
DC SUPER FRIENDS
SUPER FRIENDS
HERO

Solve the maze to help Batman track down the Riddler. Watch out for the Joker and Bane!

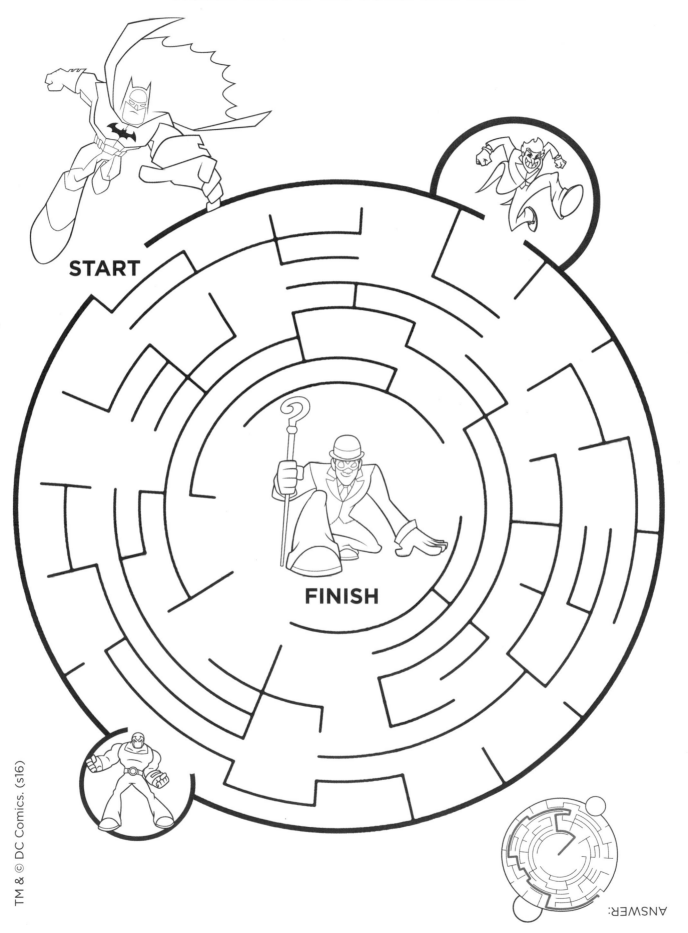

START

FINISH

ANSWER:

Help these heroes defeat the villains!
Circle the good guys, and put an X over the bad guys.

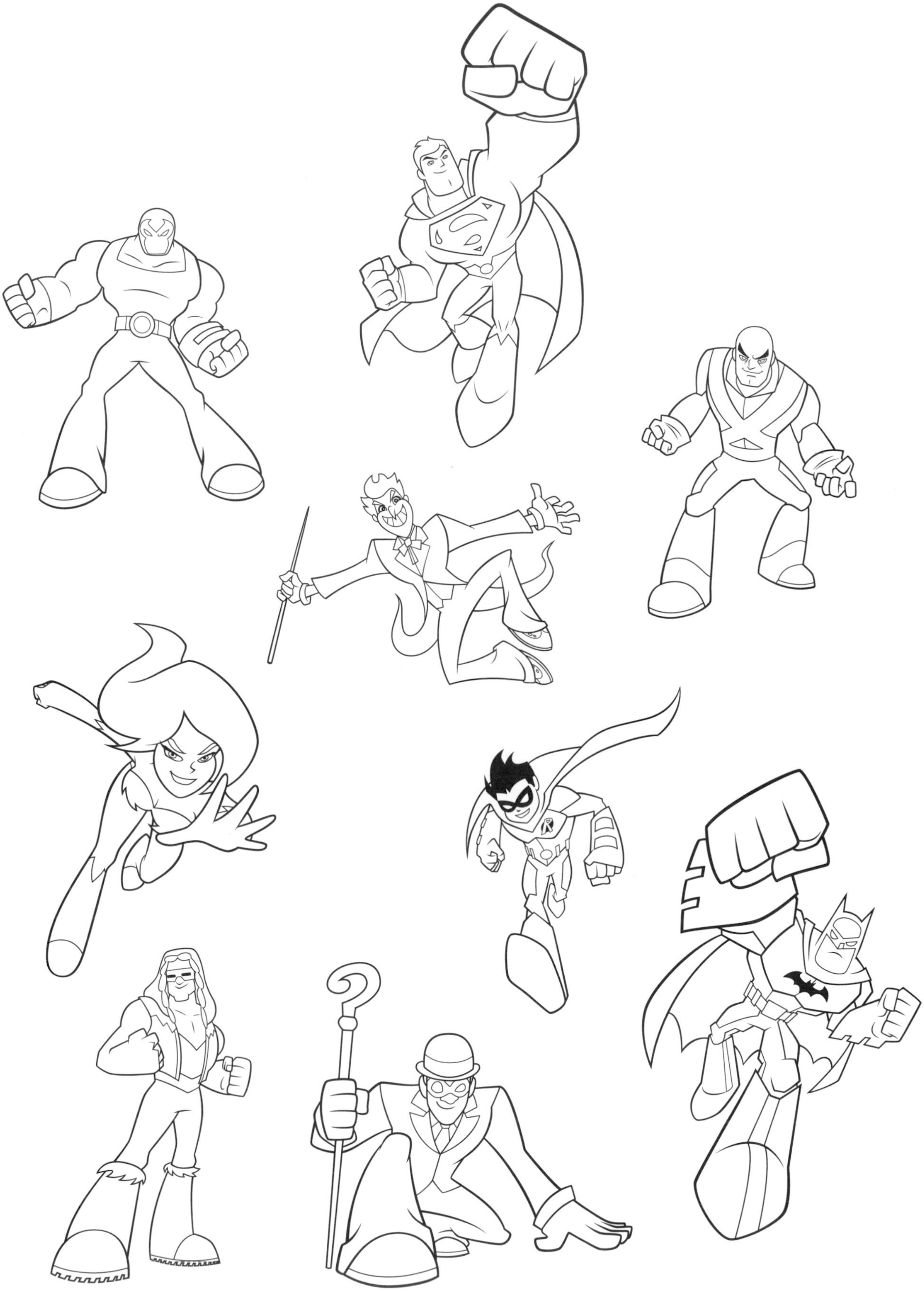

To learn the name of this well-dressed villain, follow the lines and write each letter in the correct box.

N U P T E N E G I H

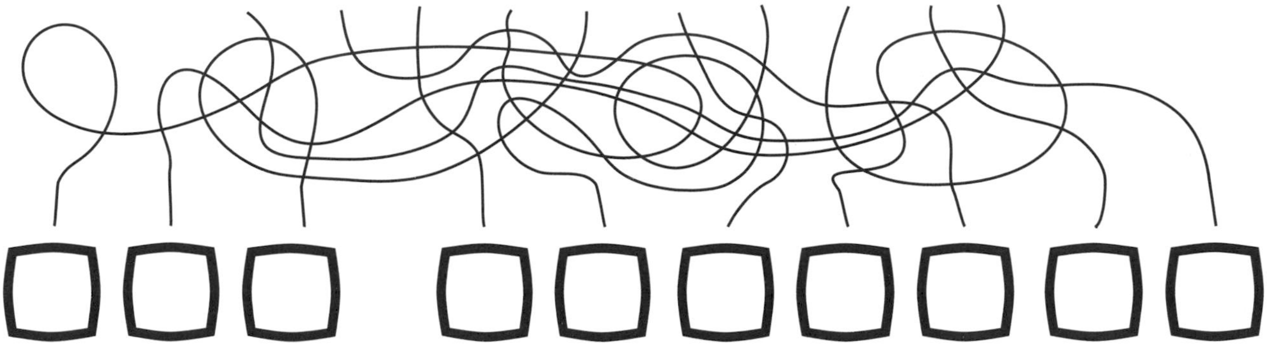

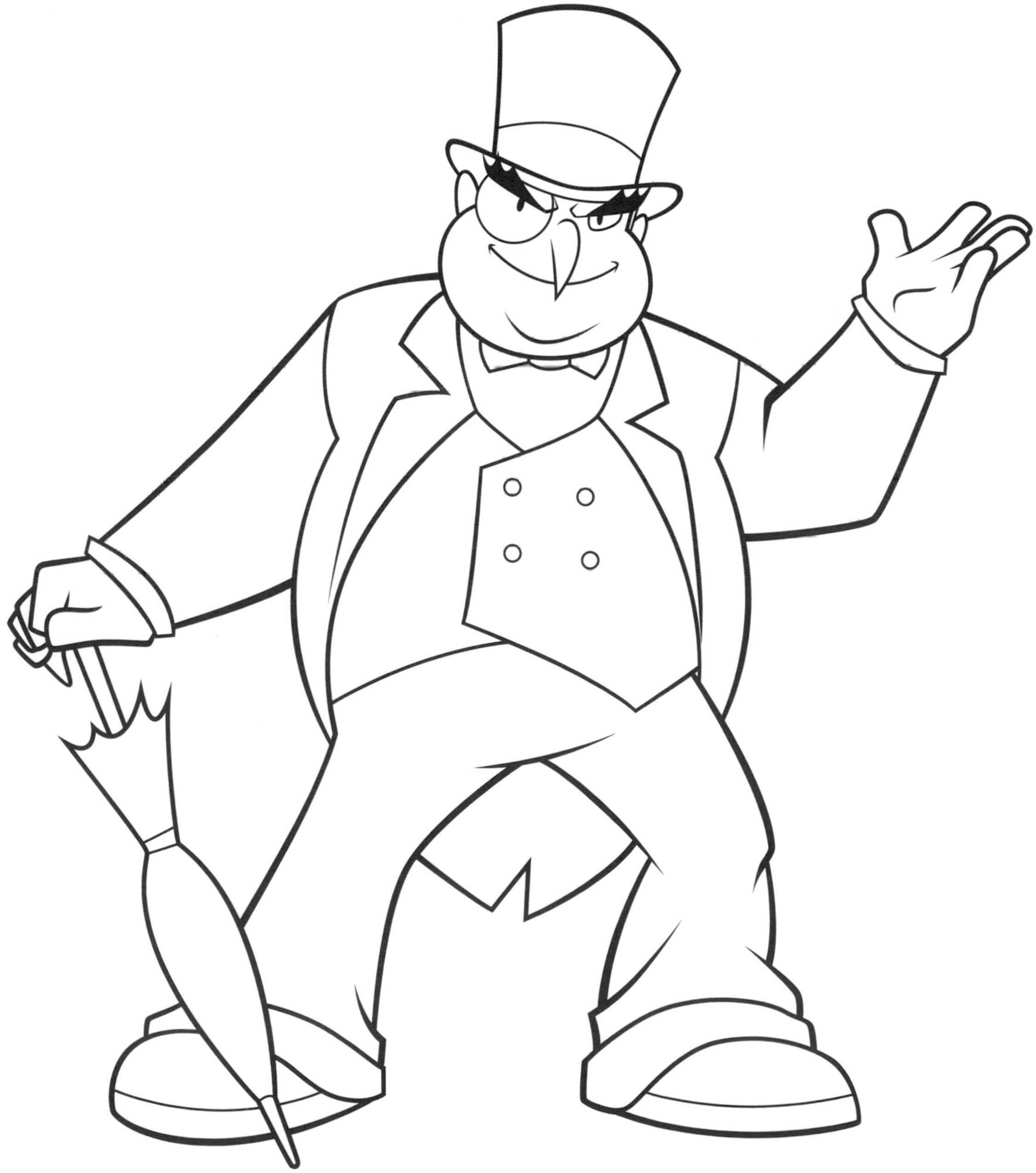

ANSWER: The Penguin.

The Penguin has lots of trick umbrellas.
How many can you count?

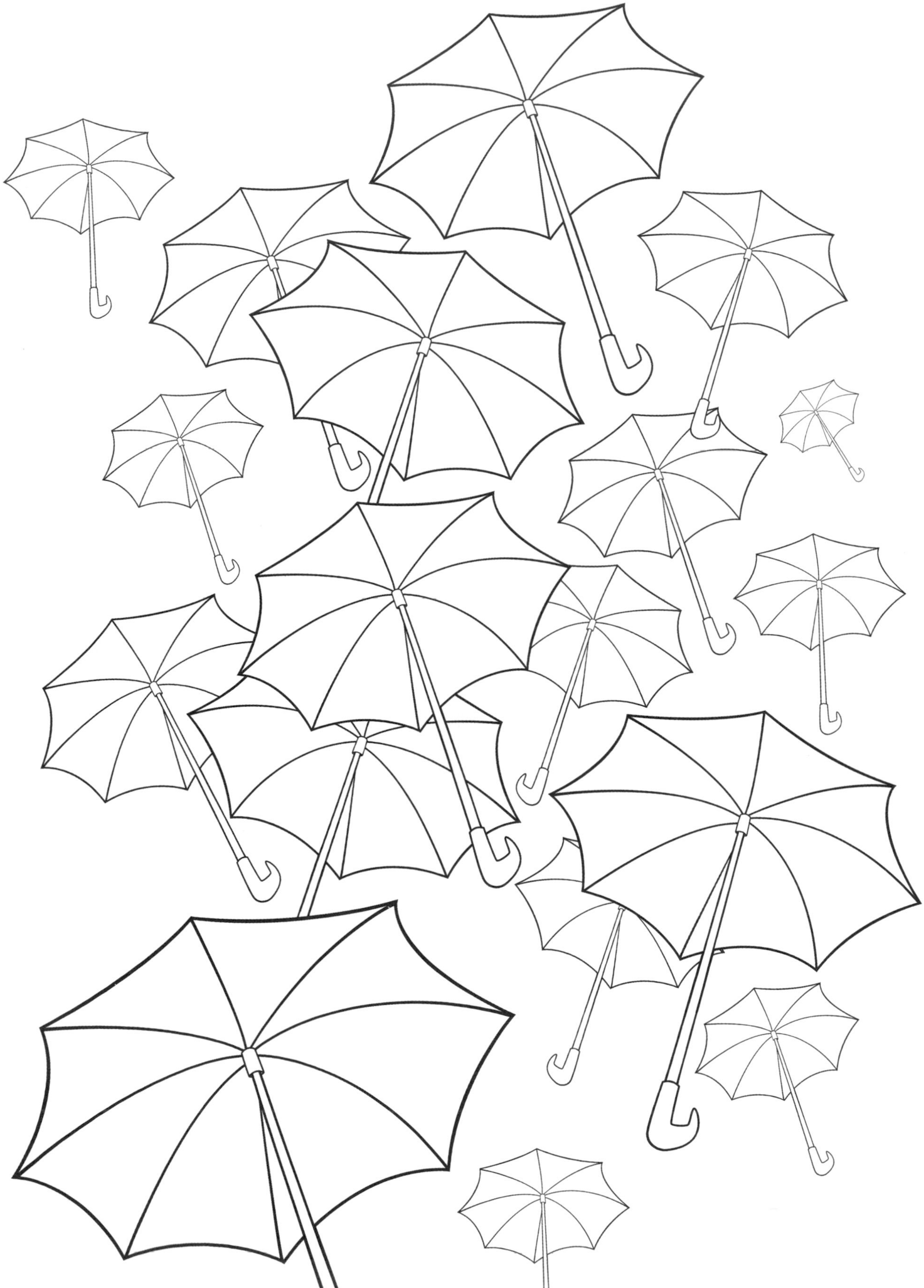

ANSWER: 18.

Complete this picture of Hawkman.

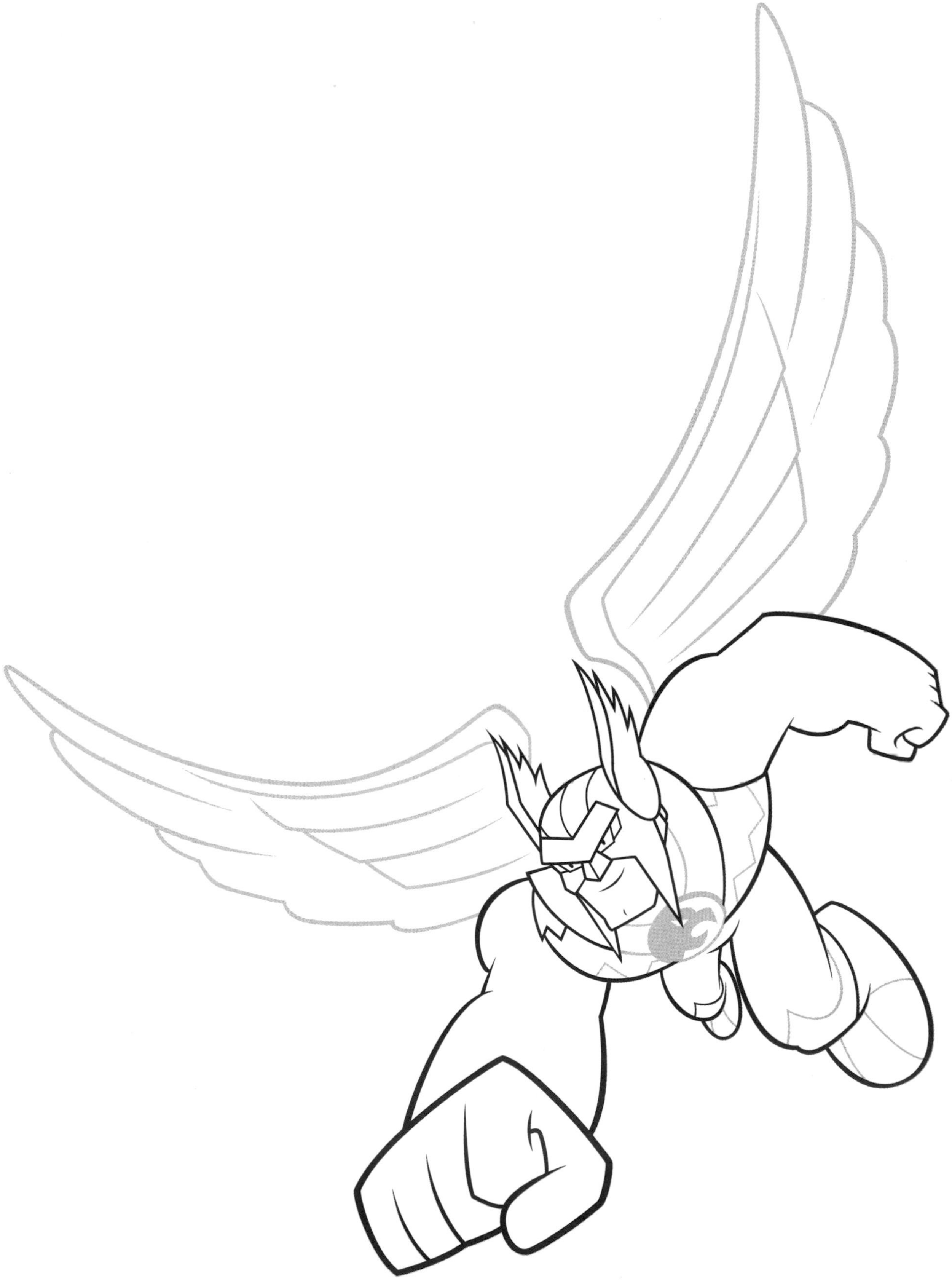

The Penguin gets the drop on the Boy Wonder!

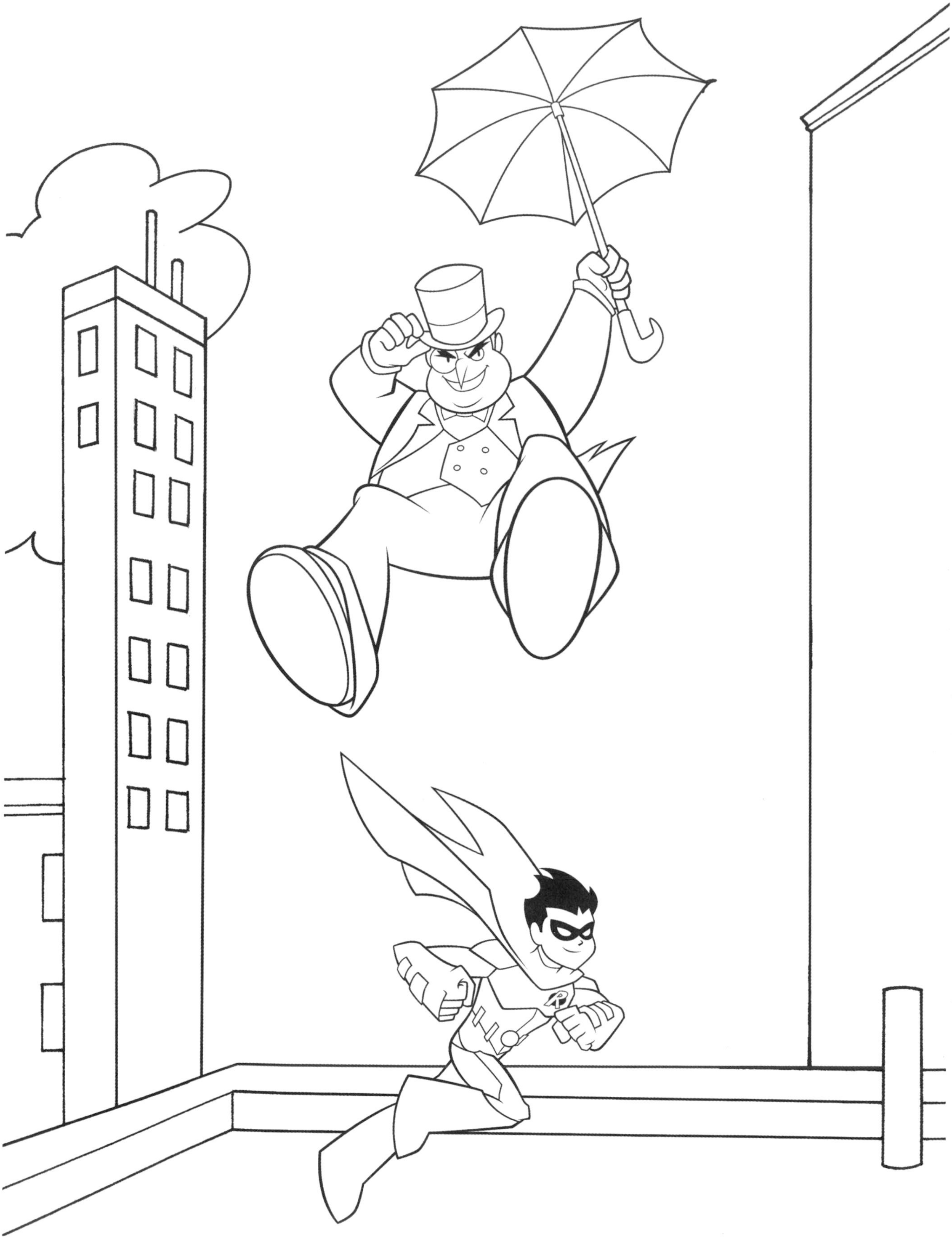

Who is this massive villain? To find out, cross out all the *Z*s. Write the remaining letters in order on the blanks.

Z S Z Z O Z L Z O Z Z M Z Z O Z N Z
G Z Z R Z U Z N Z Z Z D Z Y Z

___ ___ ___ ___ ___ ___ ___

___ ___ ___ ___ ___ ___

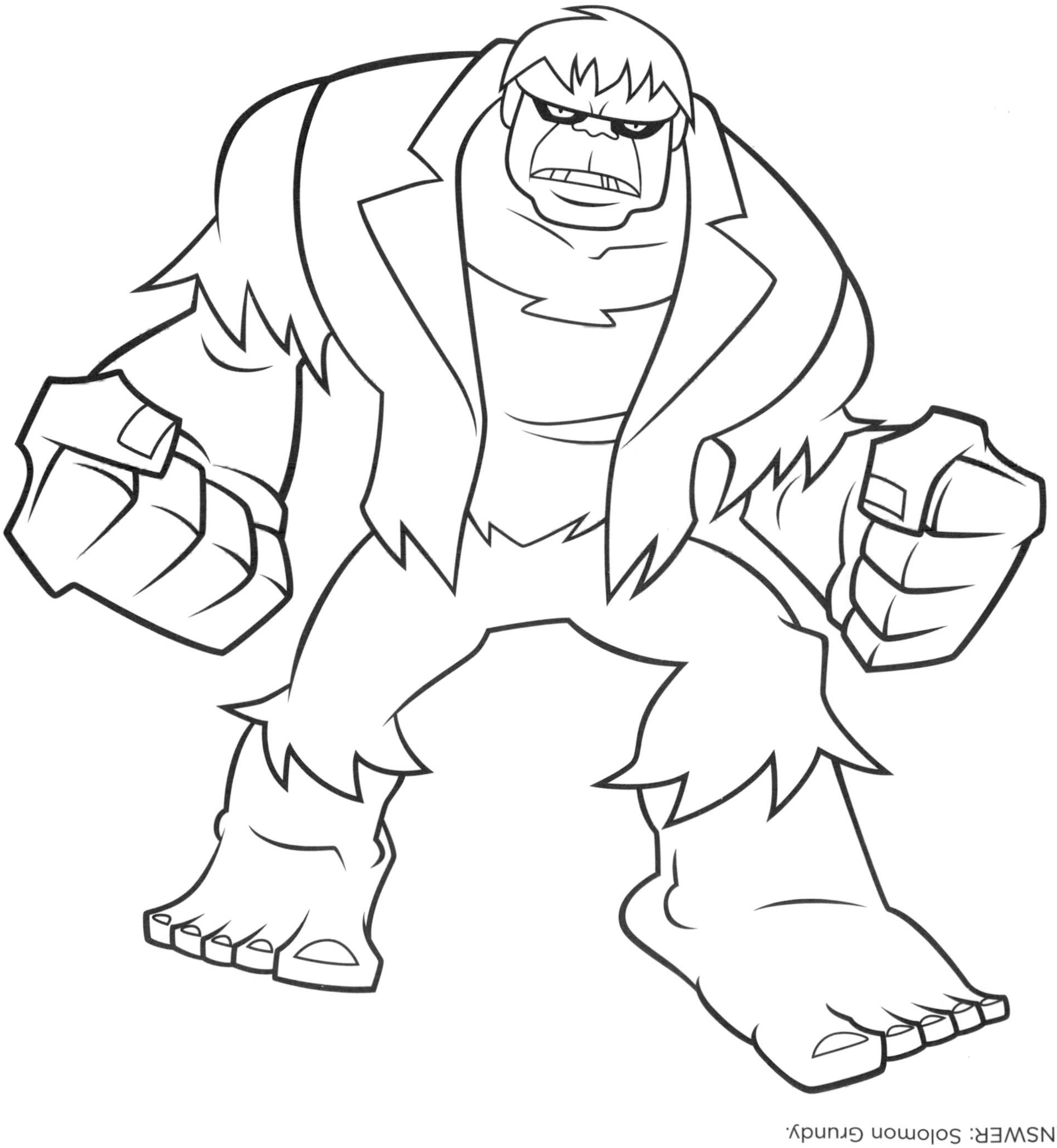

ANSWER: Solomon Grundy.

Grundy is on the loose! Help Green Lantern find him by solving the maze. Remember to steer clear of Captain Cold and Lex Luthor!

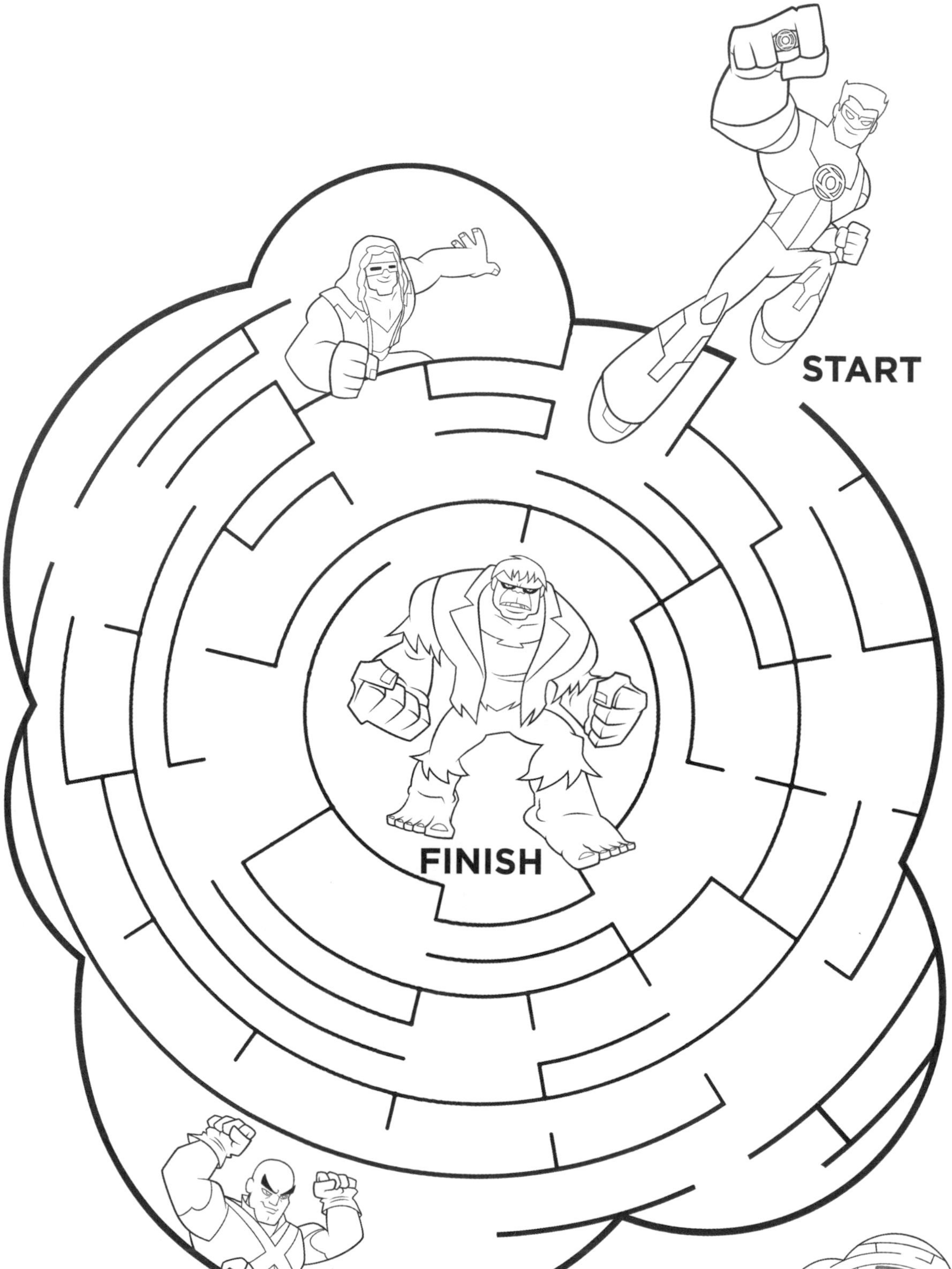
START
FINISH

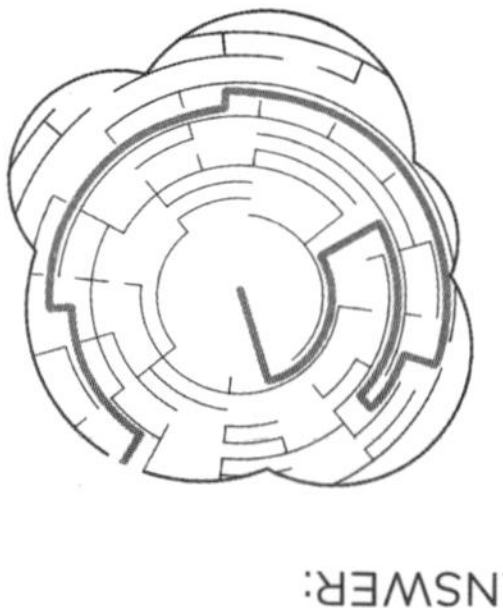

ANSWER:

To find out the name of this villain, follow the lines and write each letter in the correct box.

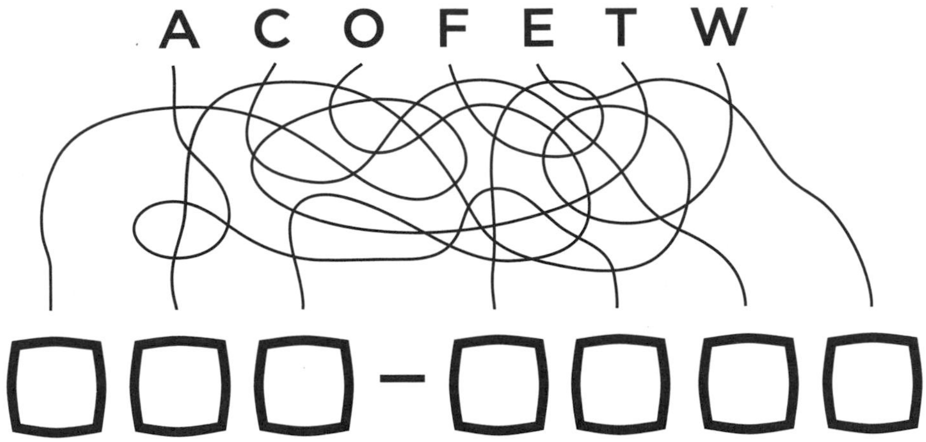
A C O F E T W

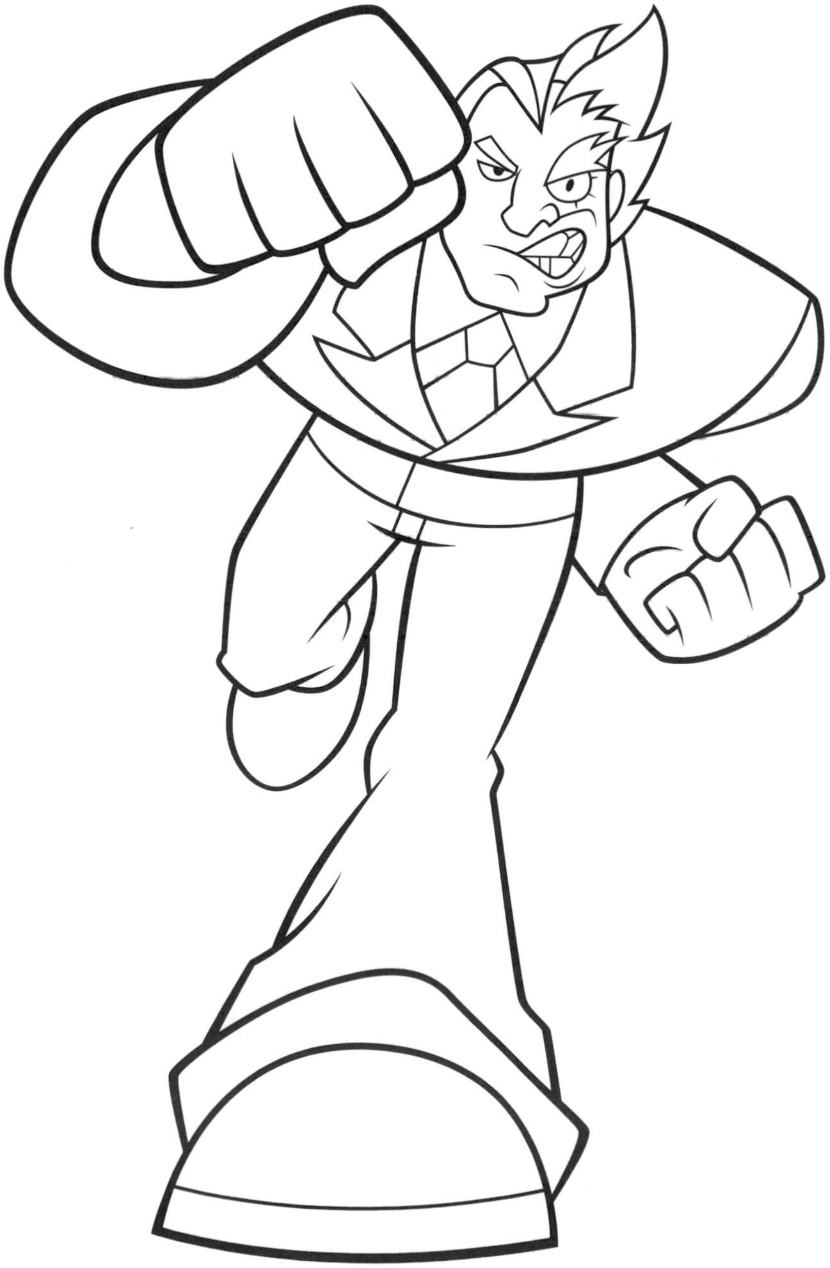

ANSWER: Two-Face.

Two-Face has too many coins! How many can you count?

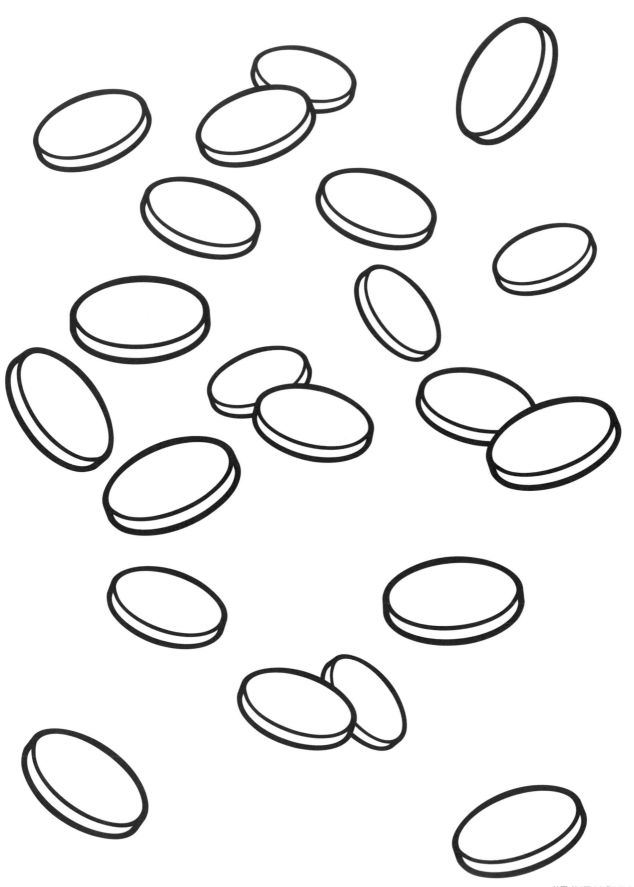

Find the shadows that match these villains' poses exactly.

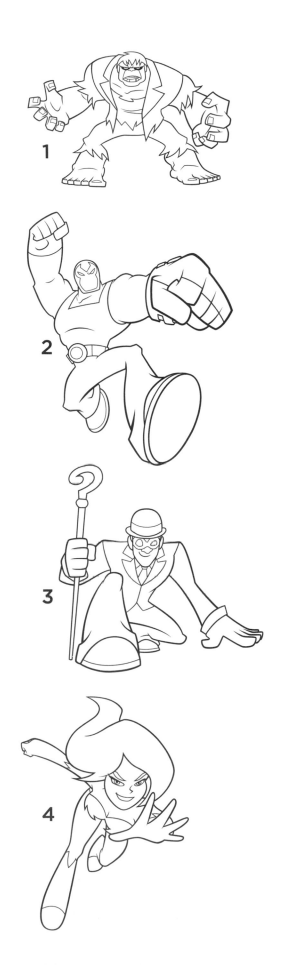

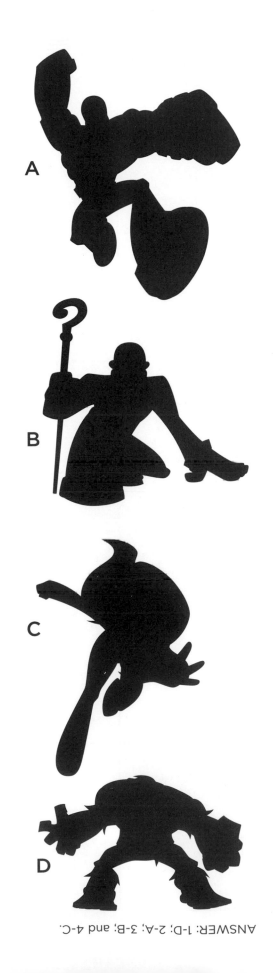

ANSWER: 1-D; 2-A; 3-B; and 4-C.

Cross out all the pictures of Two-Face and the Joker. How many pictures of Batman and Robin are left?

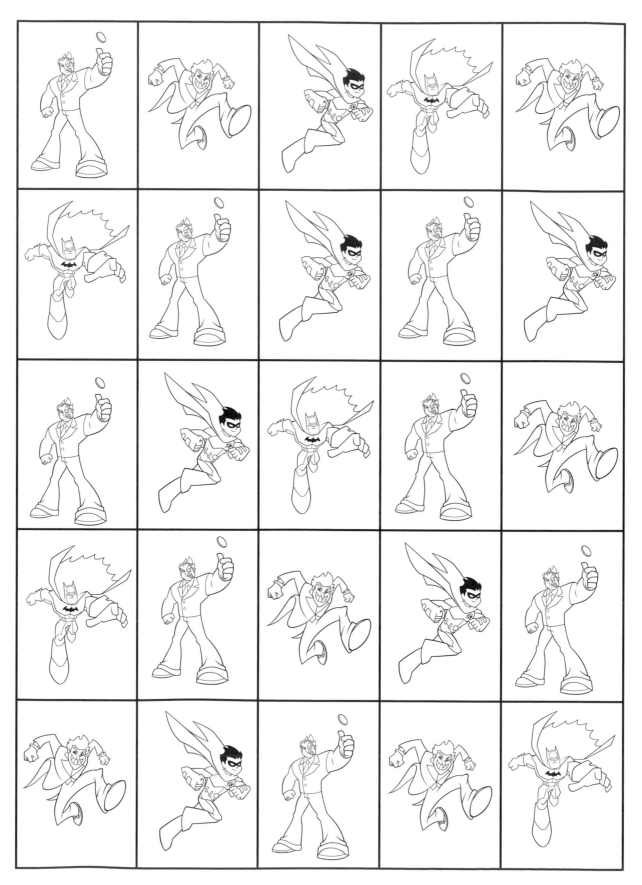

Use the code to find out the name of this backward villain.

A=1	B=2	I=3	O=4	R=5	Z=6

___ ___ ___ ___ ___ ___ ___

2 3 6 1 5 5 4

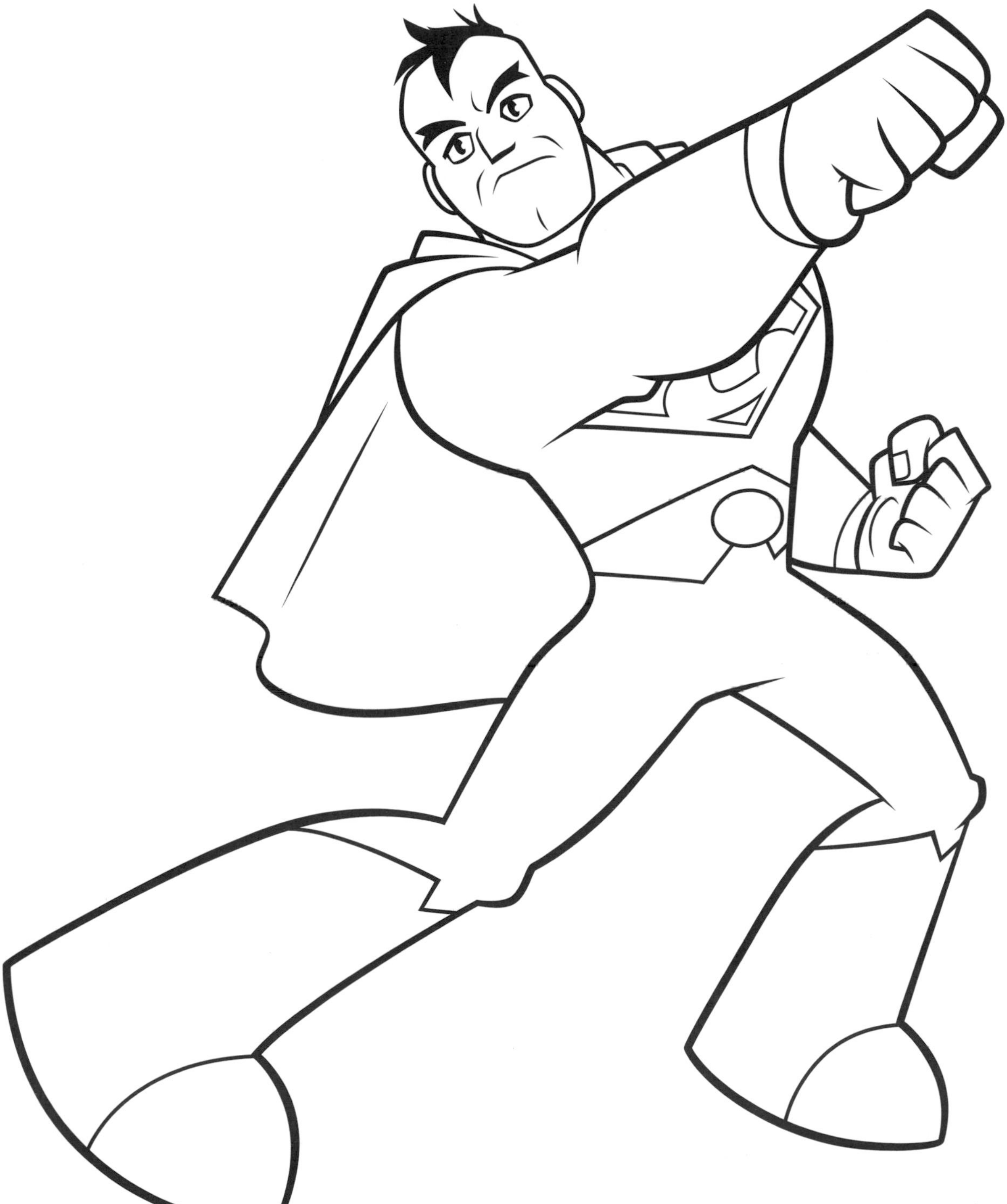

ANSWER: Bizarro.

Superman battles Bizarro!

With a friend, take turns connecting two dots with a straight line. If the line you draw completes a box, give yourself a point. If your box has Bizarro in it, give yourself two points. If your box has Superman in it, give yourself three points. When no more boxes can be made, the player with more points wins.

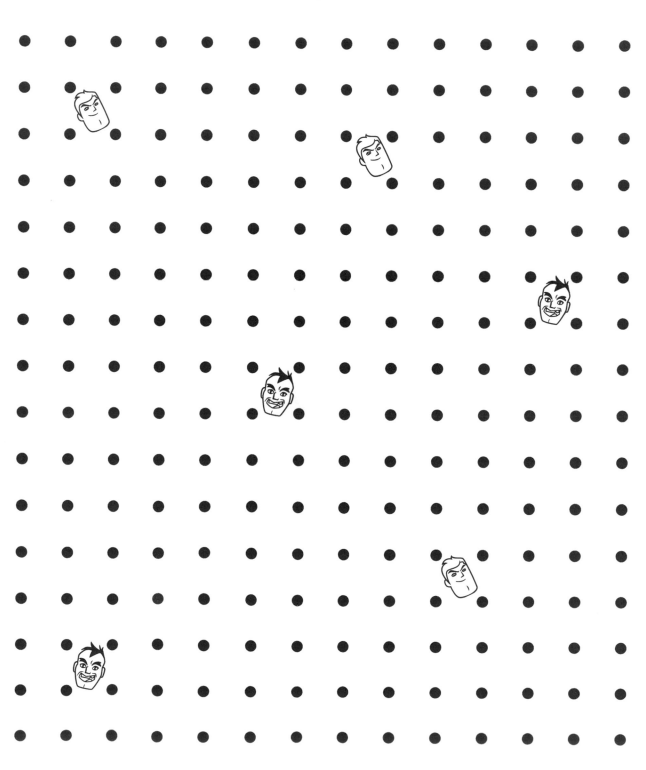

Play again!

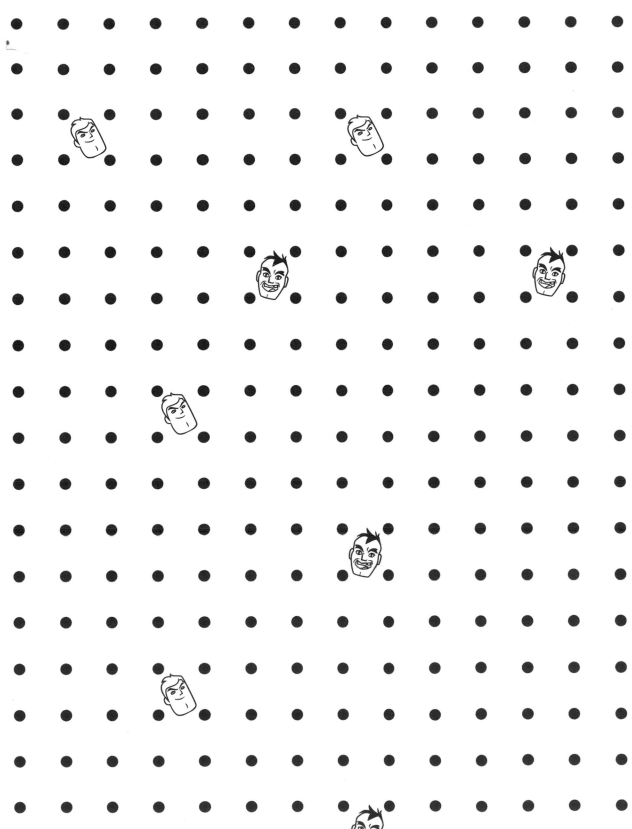

Bad guys, beware the Super Friends!

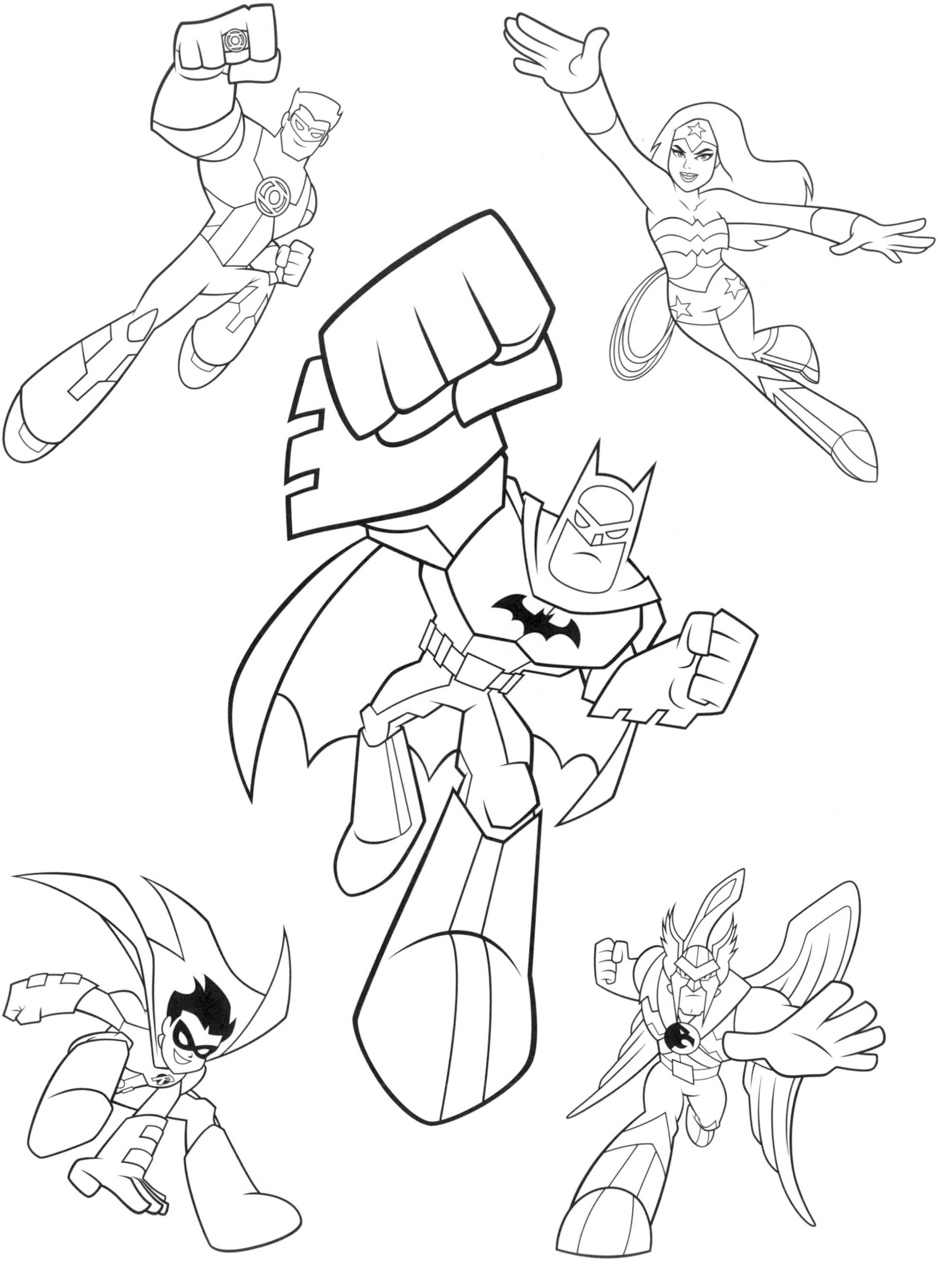

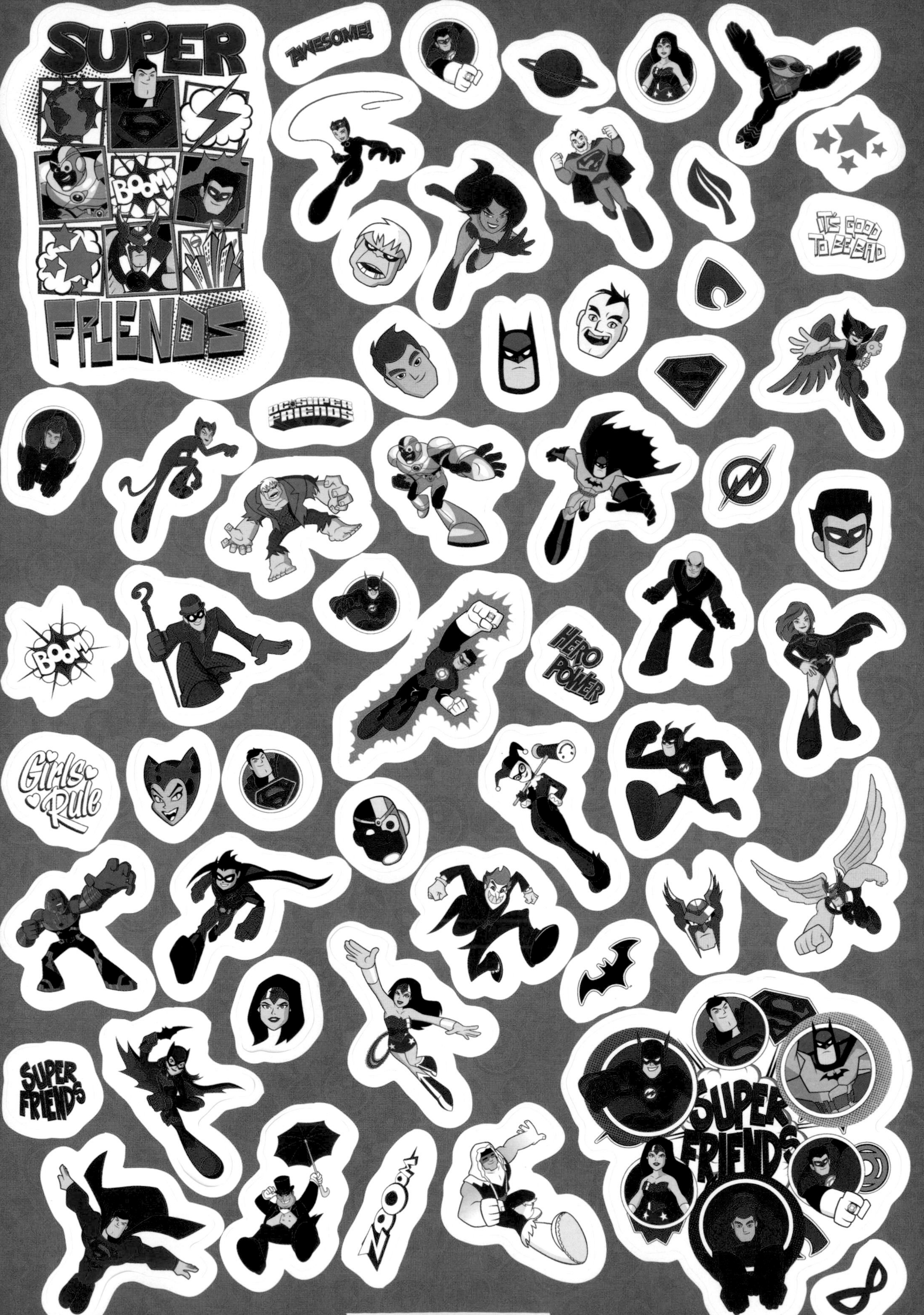
SUPER
BOOM
FRIENDS
AWESOME!
IT'S GOOD TO BE BAD
DC SUPER FRIENDS
BOOM
HERO POWER
Girls Rule
SUPER FRIENDS
ZOOOM
SUPER FRIENDS

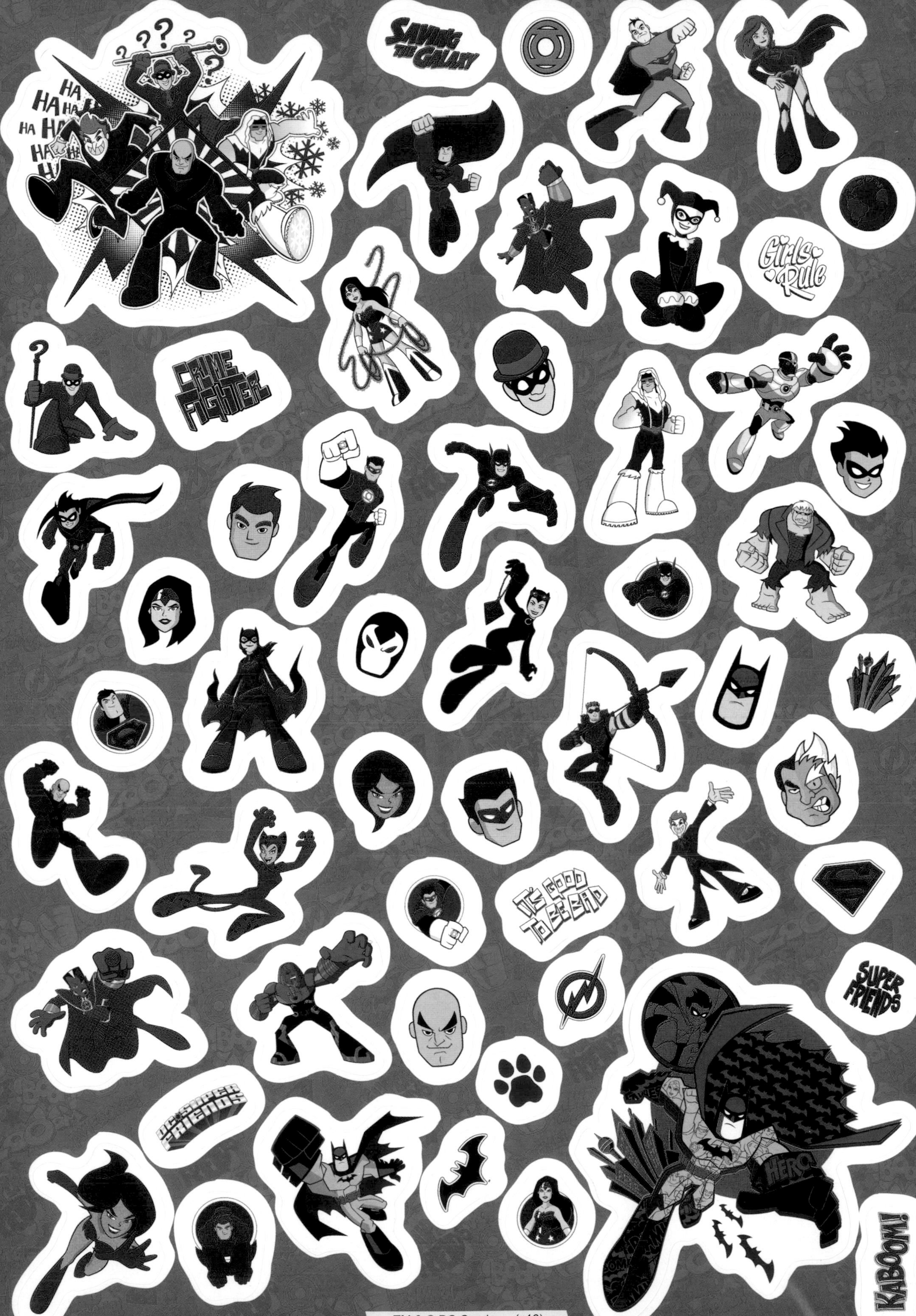

SAVING THE GALAXY
Girls Rule
CRIME FIGHTER
IT'S GOOD TO BE BAD
SUPER FRIENDS
DC SUPER FRIENDS
HERO
KABOOOM!

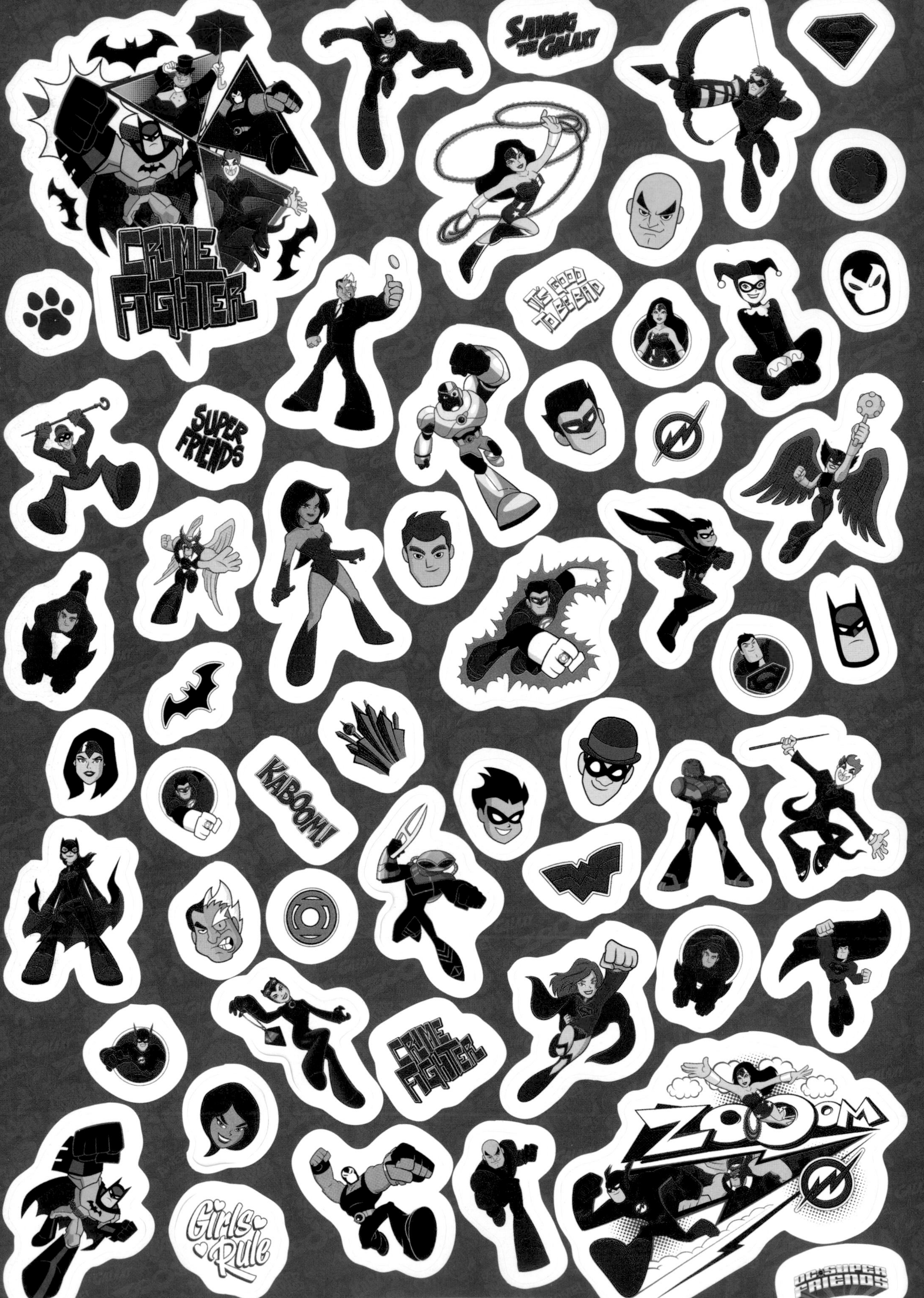
SAVING THE GALAXY
CRIME FIGHTER
IT'S GOOD TO BE BAD
SUPER FRIENDS
KABOOM!
CRIME FIGHTER
ZOOM
Girls Rule
DC SUPER FRIENDS

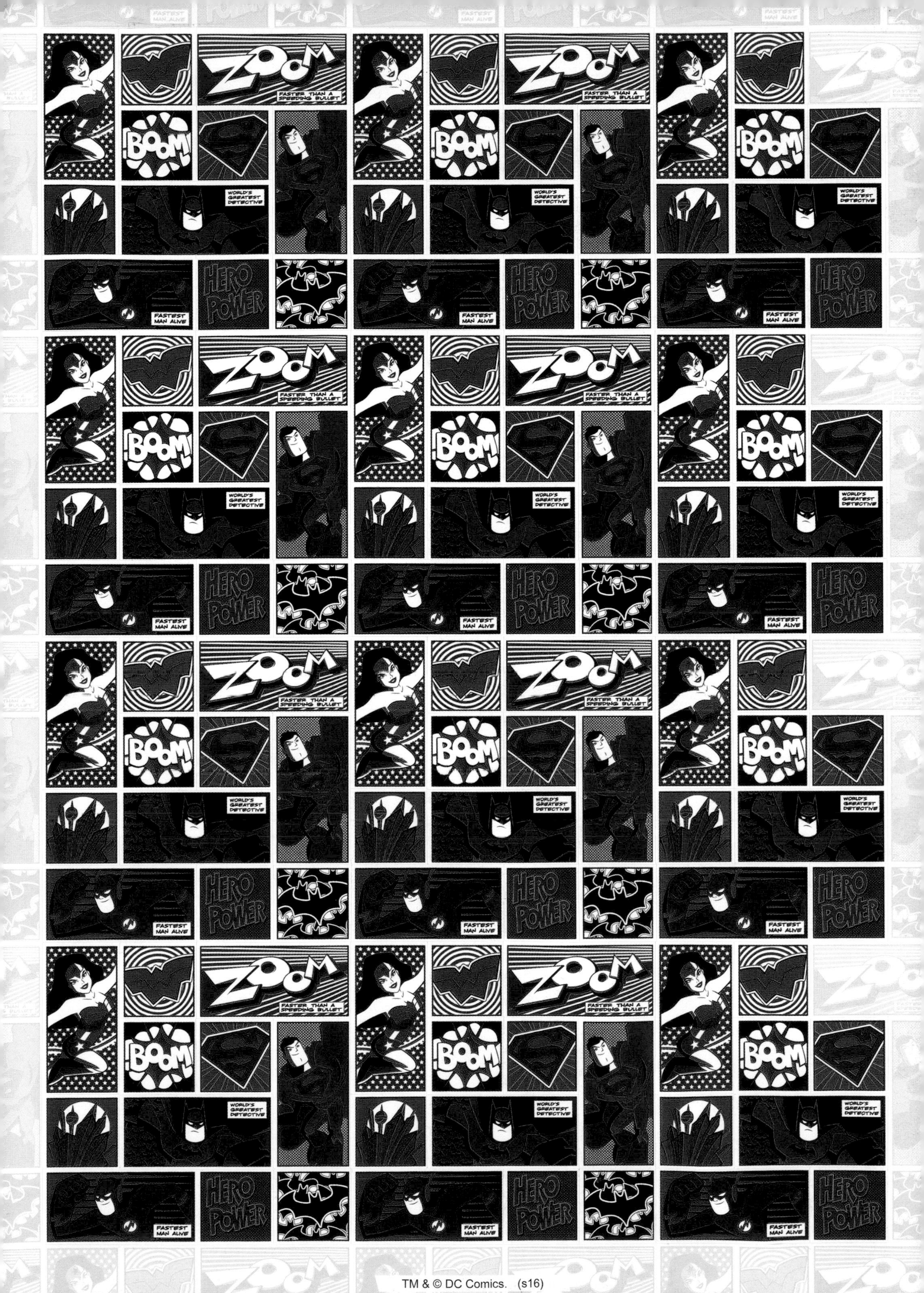
ZOOM
FASTER THAN A SPEEDING BULLET
BOOM!
WORLD'S GREATEST DETECTIVE
HERO POWER
FASTEST MAN ALIVE